Acclaim For the Work of
DAVID J. SCHOW!

"Smart, scathing, and verbally inventive to an astonishing degree, David J. Schow [is] one of the most interesting writers of his generation."
    —*Peter Straub*

"Take no prisoners fiction that rarely pulls away from the grisly heart of the matter, Schow's prose is extremely cinematic, filled with pungent dialogue, sharp, memorable characters, and a sense of macabre irony worthy of Alfred Hitchcock."
    —*San Francisco Chronicle*

"[A] sinuous psychological thriller…Schow works suspenseful sleight-of-hand with his story…His kinetic orchestration of events [and] vivid hardboiled prose push the plot to a thunderclap climax that…is a measure of coolly calculated audacity."
    —*Publish*

"Evocatively descri⋯⋯⋯⋯⋯⋯⋯⋯⋯⋯⋯⋯nks up the tension effo⋯⋯⋯⋯⋯⋯⋯⋯⋯⋯ovel is akin to being slip⋯⋯⋯⋯⋯
    —*The Ago*⋯

"Edgy, insightful, and fearless."
    —*Joe R. Lansdale*

"David Schow writes with a lethal beauty."
    —*Robert R. McCammon*

The night came alive with auto weapons fire.

"What the hell are you doing—" Carl hollered.

"Shut up. Get in the back. Head down."

Lacquer chips jumped from the hood of the Town Car as a fusillade of nine-millimeter slugs flattened into the windshield, making starbursts, rude impact hits without the attendant cacophony of gunfire.

Triangulating, Barney figured four shooters, three of them the guys after the bag. One grabbed and they all scattered two seconds before the limo came to a dust-choked halt near the natural stone foundation.

Barney already had the Army .45 in his hand.

As the car stopped he chocked his door open with his foot and stayed low, popping two rounds and dropping the runner with the bag, who was not shooting. The bag was scooped by another runner who fired back—Uzis, from the sound and cycle rate. Barney ducked the incoming angry metal bees, mostly discharged unaimed, panic fire, gangsta showoff.

The brake was up and the limo began a slow roll toward the bridge. This was intentional. Barney crabwalked along-side, scanning around for the bonus shooter, who expectedly rose from the crest of the bridge and began shooting down-ward, ineffectually. Barney put a triple-tap in his general direction to keep him down, under cover.

The right front wheel stopped against the outstretched leg of the first guy to grab the bag.

"Now," Barney shouted at Carl. "Drag that sonofabitch in here..."

GUN WORK

by **David J. Schow**

A HARD CASE CRIME NOVEL

A HARD CASE CRIME BOOK
(HCC-049)
November 2008

Published by

Dorchester Publishing Co., Inc.
200 Madison Avenue
New York, NY 10016

in collaboration with Winterfall LLC

*This book is a work of fiction. Names, characters, places, and
incidents either are the products of the author's imagination or
are used fictitiously, and any resemblance to actual events or
persons, living or dead, is entirely coincidental.*

ISBN 0-8439-5967-3
ISBN-13 978-0-8439-5967-3

Cover design by Cooley Design Lab

Typeset by Swordsmith Productions

Printed in the United States of America

Visit us on the web at www.HardCaseCrime.com

GUN WORK

Part One
The Finger House

How Barney came to occupy a room on the wrong side of management in a hostage hotel deep inside Mexico City had to do with his friend Carl Ledbetter and one of those scary phone calls that come not always in the middle of the night, but whenever you are most asleep and foggy.

"This is Carl, goddammit, *Carl*, are you there? Is that you, man? It's *you*, right?" Hiss, crackle. "Look, I don't have my cards, I don't have my ID, I don't have my passport, all I have is one of these shitty phone cards that runs out of time, they took Erica, they got her, man, grabbed her ass right out from under me, I haven't got a piss to pot, I mean a pot to piss in—"

"Carl, slow down; I'm not even awake..."

The phone pad glowed at Barney while his slowly surfacing brain tried to process information. *Anonymous Caller.*

Carl Ledbetter worked for a specialty imprint of a New York publishing house that had recently been inspired to cherry-pick non-American talent, in this case, genre novelists—science fiction, detective, horror and romance writers—and provide the best of their work in translation to US paperback audiences. Erica, whom Barney had never met, was thumbnailed by Carl as a swoony bit of red-headed business working as an editorial assistant at *Curve* magazine. They had met

at an American Booksellers Association conference,
struck sparks, fell in love, cohabitated, and had recently
begun referring to each other as fiancé and fiancée.

That was the last Barney had heard; he was not in
the habit of keeping in touch. It was nearly-forgotten
news, the kind for which you tender congratulations,
then round-file. Bad news lasted longer.

Good for Carl, Barney had thought at the time. The
whole marriage deal eliminated the thorny problem of
how to refer to your supposedly significant. *Boyfriend,
girlfriend, lover, partner, sex monkey* all seemed inadequate and socially inept for any pair of people who
were actual adults. Because of their jobs, Carl and
Erica rarely traveled together. The deal Carl's pub-
lisher wanted to cut with several rising stars of the
Mexican printed word afforded an opportunity to su-
perficially fake a vacation. From Mexico City they
could do Guadalajara or perhaps Acapulco.

Instead, Mexico City had apparently done *them*.

Barney had been keeping off the societal radar for
the last year and a half—personal travails, old stories
that don't need telling right now—and had secured a
position at the Los Angeles Gun and Rifle Range downtown in the warehouse district, occasionally working
the counter, sometimes pitching in on gun repair if the
problem was arcane enough. When you worked at a
range with a piece on your hip, every customer was
your pal from bangers to cops. It never occured to
anyone to question the legitimacy of your identity.
Guns were sexy and empowering and lots of women
begged instruction. Ample time for practice and all
the free ammo your hardware could eat. It wasn't
actual combat with real stakes, but it sufficed to fill the

in-betweens, and for a gunman it was as natural a thing as breathing free air.

Meanwhile, people tended to seek Barney's counsel whenever they fell afoul of some extralegal difficulty, the kind of gray-zone balls-up that consistently befalls people you think of as completely normal and law-abiding. Like Carl Ledbetter, who had known Barney even before they both wound up wearing dusty desert camo in Iraq. First came the reunion (*hey, it's you!*), then the wild coincidence of it all (Carl had come as a journalist with a camera; Barney as a soldier with a gun), followed by the effortless bond of de facto brotherhood between men in the same war—the kind of brotherhood that was supposed to permit, years later, the sort of advantage Carl was about to ask of his amigo.

Carl and Barney had known each other since their 20s. Carl knew somewhat of Barney's checkered past and politely never insulted his friend by asking about it. If you ever got a close look, Barney's body was peppered with old scars, the kind of wounds that never got explained. The conceits of formula story-telling would not suffice to describe him—this height, that hair, this-or-that movie actor with whatever eye color. Barney knew the value of blending; call it instinctual. To the world at large he was a stranger, a background extra quickly moving on, and he liked it that way.

Now, rate your friends, your acquaintances and your intimates. Among that group you already know which person you'd ask for help when shady badstuff rears up in your life. Yeah, *that* one—the person you always suspected was a bit illicit, a hair violent, two baby steps beyond the law. After-hours help, a less-than-kosher midnight run, some muscle, maybe some payback, and you know the person you'd call when quiet society says you should be calling a cop.

"From the top, Carl," Barney said into his phone in the dark. "Deep breaths. Simple sentences. Subject, object."

"This goddamned phone card," Carl's voice crackled back at him from one country to another. "You've got to get a phone card to use the payphones and half of them don't work. The time on the cards runs out faster than—"

"You said that already. You said they grabbed Erica. Who-they?"

In Mexico, kidnapping constituted the country's third biggest industry, after dope and religion.

"They didn't leave a business card," Carl said.

"But she was abducted."

"Kidnapped, right."

"What do they want?"

"They said a million."

"Dollars?"

"Yeah."

Barney wiped down his face. Squeezed the bridge of his nose. He didn't need to click on the nightstand lamp and become a squinting mole. "Why you?"

"Because they think I'm a rich gringo." Carl started breathing more shallowly and rapidly on the other end of the line. "My god, bro, how can I—"

"Don't start that," Barney overrode. "You were doing just fine. Calm. Calm." A beat, for sanity. "So…are you?"

"Am I what?"

"Rich. Can you cough up seven figures?"

Another beat. Barney frowned. His long-lost friend was wondering whether to lie.

Finally, Carl said, "Yeah. Don't ask how."

"And you want what from me, exactly? They've got the hostage and you've got the ransom. So, trade."

"It stinks, amigo. It stinks like underbrush when you probe by fire." He was playing the war-buddy card again. "Probing by fire" was when you cut loose a few rounds into unknown territory. If return fire erupted, you knew the hide was enemy-occupied. It helped to be fast-footed in such circumstances. The suspense was gut-wrenching, and you could smell your courage leaching out in your sweat.

"You want backup," Barney said, dreading it.

"There's nobody else I can trust in a shitstorm like this. No good faces. I'll wind up nose-down in a ditch with my money *and* Erica gone. I need your help. The kind of help you can't just buy." Another telltale beat of quiet. "Will you help me?"

Barney got Armand to feed his goldfish during what looked to be a weekend absence. He flew into Mexico City—gunless—on an ironclad passport that did not have the name "Barney" anywhere on it. Carl Ledbetter would not meet him at the airport. They had arranged a rendez in a hole-in-the-wall tapas joint that served surprisingly good *carne*, as long as you didn't question the source animal for the meat too stringently. Carl's shirt and jacket were already ringed with perspiration.

Carl *looked* like a victim.

A victim of the Zone diet, among other things. Too

much turkey in controlled portions, therefore too much tryptophan, sedating him as his life softened, knocking his guard down into comfy semi-coma. If you had to hit the gym to keep fit, you weren't moving around enough in the first place.

Carl looked like an American tourist—sideswiped by sunburn (already peeling), at sea with a non-native tongue, confused by the currency, lost without a guide. Pattern baldness, prescription spectacles and a general mien that said *mug me*. Sweating, nervous, jumpy now, ill at ease in clothing the wrong fabric for the climate; clothing which announced his outsider status to locals who grossed ten bucks a week if they were lucky.

Carl looked like a neutered tomcat. He had put on thirty pounds since hooking up with Erica. He ignored his tapas and swigged from a glass bottle of Mexican Coca-Cola loaded with real sugar, not fructose or corn syrup.

Part of the explanation he offered involved tapping the cash-flow of a rich guy on Wall Street, a broker who had learned to stash the pennies that constituted the fallout from the cups-and-balls shuffle of big money accounts. Rounded-up or down half-cents and quarter-cents from millions of dollars in invisible transfers. The crimes of which the broker was guilty already constituted more than a single-spaced page of malpractice, but it explained where Carl had been able to score his million on short notice and without suffering a credit check. The story smelled flimsy but Barney knew that was all the exposition he was going to get on that front, at least for now.

What Barney wanted was a drop plan, or shadowy faces he could track. Instrumentality, not cryptography.

At the same time, Barney hated himself for re-evaluating his old buddy Carl. There is a nasty section of the human heart: everyone has it, some people flaunt it, and it is never flattering. The *I-told-you-so* impulse. That was what Barney was feeling now, but vaguely, not wishing to confront it head-on. Carl had gotten legitimate. Hooked up with Erica, who by all reports was splendid. Then blundered into a zone of hostiles like a tyro and gotten blindsided, worse than a damned tourist. Carl had forgotten or ignored the rules of engagement. He had exposed his throat to a sharpened world.

Never, thought Barney. *Never would I get foxed like that.*

And at the same time as that same-time, Barney felt powerful and enabled. The weaknesses of guys like Carl permitted guys like Barney to exist and perse-vere. Barney could fix things. Lots of people can't fix a leaky faucet. Even more people had no idea how their automobile worked; it's just a magic box, you get inside and it goes. Barney could strip an engine or put a drop of solder into an iPod and make the magic thing *go* again.

The tough part, really, was surfing the waves of emotional garbage people brought to their problems as extra baggage, to prove how human and normal they were. You were supposed to sympathize and coddle. None of which had anything to do with fixing the problem.

So it came as a surprise when Carl whipped out a dirty kerchief and displayed a woman's severed finger with an engagement ring on it. Supposedly the dia-mond was non-conflict.

"I've looked at this a thousand times," he said, not meaning the ring. "I don't have to. It's Erica's." His expression had the dull infinity focus of someone who has been overloaded with too much truth.

"The cut looks three days old," said Barney. You could tell from the way the flesh desiccated. Lividity. Whether the amputation was rough or precise. A dozen details Barney thought he could spare Carl just now.

Carl nodded. Yep, three days. Most abductions at this price took about a week to play out.

"What else did they give you?"

Carl dug out a cellphone. "I'm supposed to call them if things screw up. Otherwise I'm supposed to wait for this thing to ring."

Barney examined the phone. Scratch marks on the case where it had been pried open and customized—probably to route through several other countries to make it trace-proof.

"How much American cash do you have?"

"You mean besides the—?" Carl's face went cheesy at almost blurting out big money while surrounded by hungry foreigners. He lowered his voice, playing spy. "A couple thousand."

Barney held out his hand under the table and Carl passed a wad of damp currency. "Give me your hotel room key. Tell the hotel you lost it. Be ready to call them at six o'clock and say you just want to get it over with. Then find a car agency and rent a car that has a global positioning system."

"What are you going to do?"

Barney pocketed the money as absentmindedly as you'd tuck a small receipt. "Go shopping."

◦

As an anonymous outsider, it was comparatively easy for Barney to score the things he wanted: three cheap cellphones, gray-market night vision binoculars, a ex-military Colt 1911-A chambered for modern .45 caliber rounds. But he was carrying more than that. He felt the crush of obligation on his shoulders, trying to weary him prematurely. He felt depressed about becoming the designated tough guy, and therefore devaluing Carl in his mind because Carl was reluctant to soldier up. At least Carl fit into the universe; all Barney had to fall back upon was rusty old myths about the nobility and honor of samurai, or ronin, or paladins—those stiff-lipped protectors who always wound up dead when the status was returned to quo.

In another way, it wasn't Carl's perceived weakness so much as Erica's influence. Erica, the yet-unseen, had changed Carl. Perceived as feminine and thus victim fodder, she was the prime target. Carl was responding as protector—a damnable predictability. If the kidnappers had grabbed Carl and pushed Erica through this wringer, things might have sorted out differently.

Barney wondered about Erica while he field-stripped and cleaned the .45. The sidearm was narrow and heavy, its parts scuffed with wear and burnished by time, but as a functional assembly of parts it was nearly indestructible. You could hammer nails with it, dunk it in fresh concrete, and it would still fire reliably. Not subtle, it would kick like a piston. It was like a long-distance mace, designed for one to fire at full arm extension, single-handedly, and knock down enemies out of choking range. The two-handed grip amateurs had learned from the movies was strictly boutique, a precious formality that made you seem more impressive on the shooting range. It was useful for target shooters; less practical in combat. Felt recoil was only a downside if you let it disrupt your aim.

The gun was an unsung classic, most definitely an antique. It was stamped UNITED STATES PROPERTY M1911A1 U.S. ARMY on the right side of the receiver, though the serial numbers had been scratched off both the slide and receiver (probably with a Dremel, Barney noticed). It bore the Coltwood plastic grips introduced in the 1940s—dull reddish-brown, no mold numbers—to replace the Coltrock and checkered walnut stocks of earlier iterations. Slide marks and factory stamps indicated the barrel had probably been replaced several times.

Barney put fifty rounds through the pistol to warm it up and check its balance. The action was tight as a snare drum; whoever had stolen or bought or recovered this pistol had taken good care of it. Barney dum-dummed another box of fifty and loaded four clips of nine. He acquired a brown leather shoulder holster that had gone furry at the rivets, with a counterbalance web for the extra magazines. He was strapped to several pounds of shooting iron plus about a pound each for the mags; the Zen trick now was to forget the burden existed. It had to become part of him, no second thoughts, and a weapon was a tool, and you never drew it capriciously. Unholstering the gun had to be instinctive, and deployment of firepower a foregone conclusion. The combination of thoughts and actions required for threat/response/aftermath was too cluttered to permit linear logic. It had to be almost autonomic, like breathing or blinking. Barney had spent a great portion of his life subverting his fear triggers in order to fix things, to get jobs done, to never flinch.

He had become, he realized, a kind of monster to normal human congress, like a rattlesnake in a society of rodents. Normally they were prey, and left you alone due to your threat protocols. Your look, your attitude, your aura. But occasionally they could gang up on you and kill you for being different. A fellow Barney would always remember as the Old Assassin had once told him: *"I am what I am, and that's not always very pretty. But being ugly is better than being nothing."*

The Old Assassin was no longer alive. He was no longer anything.

Most American law enforcement had switched to nine-millimeter sidearms in the 1980s. Not so with the ostentatiously Kevlared policemen of the Distrito Federale, who packed whatever they wanted, including grease guns dating back to the Second World War. They peppered the streets in pairs and quartets, spoiling for trouble from behind mirrored sunglasses and body armor, defining corruption in a freefire zone of aching poverty. For the most part they were sadistic, bored, and sailing on some form of speed, with a predator's eye for weaklings in any herd. This was why Carl had not called the cops, and had called Barney instead.

Carl was a tourist. Tourists were prey. End of story.

Tourism was shallow people attempting to sample local flavors that by definition were ruined by the presence of tourists. These days, it was even worse if you were an American; they openly sneered at you in

foreign ports because you were a loathsome example
of the worst of the phylum; ignorant, loud, alien,
greedy for things you cannot have, eternally disappointed in ways you can never cognate or admit.
Tourists flew the big red flag that read *victimize me, I
deserve it*.

And Mexico…Jesus. Most Americans viewed Mexico
the way most Californians viewed Tijuana, as a cesspool, a whorehouse, a dumping ground, a party zone
where you did not have to clean up after yourself.

Barney's test, and indeed his skill, was invisibility in
the midst of the circus of human congress, no matter
what country he was in. He had enough Spanish to ask
questions, order food, or obtain the odd *farmacia*
medication. *Ampicilina, cincocientos milligramas, por
favor*.

Hence, he had been able to obtain his toys without
comment.

He knew his old buddy Carl probably thought
Barney had evolved into some kind of black ops badass. Kill a man with a paper napkin. Eat roadkill to
survive. Make bombs out of fertilizer and kitchen
cleaning products. The emotional depth of a robot.
Barney was none of the inhuman things ordinary
people assumed. He was one thing—a gunman, the
sort of man who would not mind if every single
walking citizen was packing a legal firearm. It certainly
would make strangers more polite in mixed company.
To a certain extent, Barney felt that he was the embod-
iment of his own skills, an instrument for action that
could rust through disuse or neglect. For Carl to ask
Barney for help confirmed Barney's own existence.
Simple.

◦

The vehicle Carl had procured was pretty amazing.

His "rental" turned out to be an armored limousine, actually a Town Car with the stretch deck, a bomb shell underbelly, solid rubber anti-deflating tires, a personnel-carrier suspension for the extra weight, and bulletproof tinted windows.

"They had *three* of these things," Carl said rather sheepishly. "They made me a deal."

"Soft market?" said Barney.

Carl shrugged. "Look, it's got the GPS. I thought, it couldn't hurt, right?"

"As long as it goes over sixty on the flats."

Barney spent the next hour or so dismantling the map-tracker. He had watched one of his shooting range regulars do this once and retained the knack of learning and extrapolating through observation. You never knew what weird skills you might need someday. Then he performed surgery on the nylon cargo bag in which Carl planned to store his million bucks in cash. It was big. A single banknote, no matter what the denomination, weighs a gram. If the $1,000,000 had been in one dollar bills, it would have weighed over a ton. In fifties, forty-four pounds; in hundreds, half that. A million bucks in reasonably clean, circulated bills only fit into a slim Halliburton briefcase in the movies.

Barney stitched the tiny microprocessor board behind the thick vinyl logo riveted to the bag, honestly the only place to hide it.

"Do you really need to have that gun?" said Carl, eying the .45.

Barney looked at his friend as though he had just

stepped out of a flying saucer. Waited. Then, calmly:
"Yes. I need it."

"Damn, it's…heavy."

Barney's hand lashed out like a striking cobra, slamming Carl's wrist to the table. Pure instinct. He had
looked up from his work to see the muzzle of the pistol
directed at his face. Now it was angled at the ceiling,
potentially bad for other guests.

It was like a bad joke version of Barney's range test
for newbies. Hand them an unloaded piece and see
where they wave it. A good quick way to discover who
might or might not handle a firearm responsibly. Carl
had just failed with flying colors, picked up a loaded
weapon, put his finger on the trigger without thinking,
and pointed it right at Barney. The only thing he had
not done was try to imitate Cagney and make little
pchew-pchew gunshot noises…which would have been
obliterated by the sound of the weapon discharging
and spreading Barney's inmost thoughts all over the
water-stained wallpaper of their amenity-less hotel
room.

Carl stammered, "Oh, shit, I'm *sorry*, man, I—"

…*haven't held a gun in twenty years, yeah, I know.*

Barney never felt sorry for ordinary folks, regular
citizens, the law abiders, the walking dead. But sometimes he did pity them. Carl had put weapons handling,
and Iraq, far behind him. Even there, Barney remembered him with an AR-15, mostly for show, but never a
handgun.

Carl was frittering, nervous with anticipation. He
needed a chore.

"Have you got a picture of Erica?" said Barney,
stowing the gun, which had been cocked and locked.

Suddenly it was very important for Barney to obtain

a mental image of the person they were supposed to rescue. He certainly wasn't going to get an accurate account from Carl. Too much emotion polluting the information. Barney needed to see a photo.

Predictably, the snapshot Carl produced was from the humid depths of an overstuffed wallet. At least he hadn't stored a thousand pictures of his beloved on his phone or iPod.

Erica Ledbetter, née Erica Elizabeth Stolyer, appeared to be a gamine redhead with Bombay Sapphire blue eyes and a wide, generous mouth; pure Midwestern corn-fed all-Americano hotcha; the girl who had fled the small town for better things. Because she was standing beside Carl in the photo, Barney put her height at about five-four, give or take heels. Something in the glint of those eyes gave Barney the feeling that she was very camera-conscious, and always tilted her head down and looked up when there was a lens present. It did not make her look older but did make her look dangerous beyond her apparent youth; Carl had mentioned that she was currently thirty-three years old. Fair complexion; freckles. No wonder they had snatched her. She could not have looked more out-of-town, a pale, white, well-appointed, red-headed target.

Beyond the image, here is what Barney saw: *She used to date outlaws but tired of their arrested adolescence. Probably snagged a useless college degree or two. Just old enough, now, to appreciate adult company. Doesn't want children and never has; that DNA imperative was subtracted from her makeup, so this woman has sex for pleasure.* Barney looked at Carl again, now seated on a sagging twin bed redolent of mildew, staring uncomprehendingly at a TV game show in Spanish. A lot of people were shouting and talking very fast. Carl would have to work to satisfy this woman.

Back to the photo: *The type of woman who does not expect convenience, knows life entails pain, and earns what she considers to be her rewards.* Yeah: If held captive, she could probably muster some backbone. A darker thought: *Maybe her union with Carl was strategic.*

First impressions, a still life, impossible to say.

Barney handed Carl one of the cellphones. "The ringers are off. They'll blink. These are our walkies."

"What's the third one for?"

"I put the guts into the car's GPS, which is a simple receiver. Now it'll tell us where the chip is, instead of where the car is."

"You mean where the bag of money is. Why? If they give Erica back when we—"

Barney overrode him. "If they don't, we've got something to follow. If they're smart, they'll ditch the bag straightaway. The difference could be just enough time. A fix, a location, a general direction. I mean, you're not going to be able to Google 'hostage hideouts' and come up with a list of addresses."

"You still want me to call them tonight?"

"Yes."

Whatever Barney was going to add was cut short by a knock on the door, in a place where there was no room service.

Nobody was supposed to know where Carl and Barney were headquartered. Barney had engineered the move himself, advising Carl to keep his original hotel room at a place six blocks distant. Nobody was supposed to know Barney was an added extra guest, and it was a fair bet that housekeeping was not this formal, not at the dive Barney had purposefully selected.

The gun was already in Barney's grasp as he backed toward the bathroom. With a finger of silence to his lips, he directed Carl toward the door.

Here is a snapshot of what walked in:

Long legs on six-inch heels, liquid brown eyes, skin the color of Bailey's Irish mocha, shiny gaze, glittering bangles, sharp edges, a halter top and skirt that pretty much showed you in detail what you were getting—a healthy balcony (no implants), good teeth, a few scars for character and no scabs—along with the triple-shot of attitude that stormed into their presence. From what Barney could figure out from his vantage, eavesdropping, this flamboyant vision's name was Estrella—"star."

"Hey, Carlito," she said, advancing on Carl. "You should know better than to try and hide from your *chamaca*…you alone?"

Her radar was good, as if she could smell Barney in the space, and Carl knew better than to try faking it. "Ran into an old war buddy."

Barney had been cast in the part, no audition, and now the spotlight was on. He flushed the toilet to give himself an entrance cue. It gurgled and tried to back up. The bowl was ringed with brown stains similar to the strata of calcification on the teeth of many Mexican citizens, a fringe benefit of no fluoride. Estrella obviously enjoyed a better dental plan.

"Hey," Barney said, playing his walk-on badly. "Company?"

"*Hombre*," said the intruder, inviting enough but not game for a handshake. She sized Barney up in an eyeblink. "Looks like *you're* the company."

Barney tried to picture the pie chart of her bloodline, which looked to be a generational dime-a-dance mix of Latin, Asian, maybe some Dutch, plus a shot of some indefinable exotic extra wallop.

Great. Carl had gotten himself entangled with some Mexican hottie. The scenario sucked more by the microsecond. She needed to be jettisoned.

"You come to party with Carlito?" She wagged her eyebrows up and down.

"Just *cervezas* and dirty boy talk," Barney said. But there was no beer in the room.

"You gonna talk dirty to me, Carlito?" She already had her hand on his belt buckle, pulling him into a clinch. Possessive. Territorial.

"You guys need a moment?" Barney smiled. It hurt his face.

Estrella held up two fingers. Peace sign. "Two moments."

Barney's gaze exchanged information with Carl's: *You okay?*

Carl: *Yeah. Let me deal with this.*

"I'll just go get some cigarettes," Barney said. He didn't smoke. The gun was beneath his shirt, against his spine, as he exited.

There are little *mercados* and *bodegas* all over the city, but if you are smart you don't pop out to pick up drinks and a snack after nightfall, at least without bodyguards or armored support. Fearful eyes will watch you from behind curtains as you pass. Buildings are locked, bolted, barred. Surly glares from darkened portals await you, sizing you up. The air is thick with feral pheromones and incipient hazard. Teen punks, drug casualties, bangers and outright sociopaths are eager to test your *machismo*. They always mock but never kid. They are coyotes on the lookout for the next domestic pet-snack. As Barney stepped out, the sun was on the wane. About an hour before the vampires came out to enjoy *their* time.

Trouble would come later. For now, Barney knew he had nine little ballistic friends with him. Plus one in the pipe, already chambered.

He purchased some El Sol to cut the dust, Cokes, and a couple of American protein bars. He avoided the "chocolate-flavored" snacks because the dye and sea-weed used to color them tended to turn your poop green. Real Mexican chocolate was pretty wonderful, but this packaged stuff was mass-market and of questionable origin.

He wondered if Carl's cellphone would ring while he was with Estrella. Now *that* would be a French farce come to life.

He squandered about twenty minutes, stopping to watch a cart vendor expertly spatulate some simmering *chorizo* tacos. The aroma was hypnotic. The grinning brown entrepreneur had evenly spaced two-millimeter gaps between each of his teeth and the next, but his cart was scrupulously clean and his ingredients looked fresh. Some of the best food in Mexico comes from these little wheeled stands, the kind of thing that would make *turistas* grimace. Barney was tempted but decided not to weigh himself down with chow, in case he and Carl had to move nimbly later. He bought a Manzana in a glass bottle from the vendor's bin of *refrescos*; the apple-flavored soft drink was very popular down here.

Mexico was its own set of contradictions, overpopulated with Catholics mired in poverty who nonetheless gave to the church. Friendly people who would open your throat at a wrong word. Helpless people who might help you; trapped people who might free you. Rare beauty in the midst of ugliness; atrocities framed in Spanish gold. A frontier sense of liberty and advantage butted against the lowering specter of threat. Barney's image of Mexico City was summed up by the Basilica de Guadalupe—not the new, adjacent Astrodome version, but the original shrine where Juan Diego supposedly first saw the image of the Virgin in a blue mantle in 1531. Second only to the Vatican as a holy place and destination of pilgrimage, the grand old building has been sinking into the earth since the late 1960s due to faulty foundations. It was Mexico in a nutshell: most revered, gothically ornate, culturally omnipresent, sinking into the dirt in the middle of a vast city center only slightly smaller than Red Square in Moscow.

Estrella was brushing her teeth when Barney returned. She grabbed an El Sol without asking and swigged half of it. Her scent filled the room, not unpleasant, a vague waft of spice that hit you when she passed; maybe it came from all her burnished mahogany hair.

"You dinna hafta take a *vacation*, baby," she said to Barney. "We can party if you want."

"Later we will," said Barney, ever the courtly gentleman, feeling the way a nine-year-old feels when he inadvertently catches his parents in the act of making younger siblings.

She kept glancing at the door. Gotta go. They all fumbled through the usual air-filling small talk, and presently she breezed away, leaving her scent to pleasure the room.

"Half mast," Barney said, indicating Carl's zipper.

Carl secured his cargo, already anticipating Barney's actual concerns. He gulped most of an El Sol as though he had just crawled off the Gobi desert. Cleared his throat a couple of times. "It's a little…uh, complicated."

"No doubt."

Carl wiped down his face. His hand came away oily. The world was still the same. It would not erase like one of those Magic Slates.

"See…Erica had this thing when she was in New York. This affair. Right about the time she got promoted at *Curve*, the magazine. It was just one of those things, like, y'know, those trap-reactions."

"You mean she was looking down the gun barrel at marriage, which means settling, which makes everything boring, and soon you feel your youth passed you by, so you've got to bust out? One last fling?"

"It's not like she loved the guy or anything. She came clean; she was up-front about it."

"So you brought her down here either to try to zip up your relationship in a foreign port or keep an eye on her, and it's not going as well as you hoped?"

"She got *kidnapped*, man!"

"And between the time she got kidnapped and now, Estrellita bounces along to fill your lonely waiting period? What, did you run out of magazines?"

Carl flushed crimson again. "I met her in a bar. I was going out of my mind, man."

Barney sighed. They'd gone through worse, and crazier, in Iraq.

"Erica is the only thing I've ever done right in my life," Carl said. "You remember how I used to be. I was a world-class fuckup. Still am. That's why I need you. That's why I need to save Erica." He held his hands out in entreaty. "She's all I've got now."

Barney tried never to judge. What was that line about walking a mile in another man's shoes? Oh yeah: *By the time he figures out you've screwed him over, you're a mile away, and you've got his shoes.*

"Call the bad guys," Barney said.

The Rio Satanas was not a genuine river. It was a toxic spillway etched into bedrock by overflow from Mexico City's compromised waste management system. It was lost—that is to say, handily concealed—within the contaminated maze of industry on the municipal outskirts, everything from oil pumpers to propane plants contributing their discharge. At some point, somebody had built a wooden bridge over one of its tributaries, the veins and backwaters eroded by its determined march toward cleaner waterways. The bridge was almost quaint-looking, as though it had been shipped in from New England, but the whole place would never make for an attractive postcard.

The bridge was the rendez, and Carl obtained directions. Barney drove the ostentatiously ridiculous limo, even donning a chauffeur's cap he found stashed in the glovebox. Why not play it to the rim? Rich American shows up in big car driven by obvious lackey to deliver *dinero grande* with extra sauce.

Using the GPS in the car, Barney checked the signal on the transplanted chip. Thumbs up.

They got lost, naturally, trying to navigate chuck-holed streets with no signs, following directions mostly by landmark—a clear, wide, long, twisting trail that would allow ample surveillance, and guaranteed no tails or hidden reinforcements. They knew they were in the right general area when they could see the car headlights cutting through assorted noxious gases. They could *see* the air. Dark, now.

Barney scanned the perimeter a safe distance from the bridge, using the nightvision binocs. Wherever their opponents were, they had blended well. No movement, no hot spots just yet. A few heartbeats of very tense quiet, to the backbeat of distant machines, grinding, pumping, polluting.

When the cellphone went off in Carl's hand he nearly shrieked like a freshman with an icicle up his nether port.

For the first time, Barney heard the curiously uninflected voice that was bossing Carl around.

"You are to exit the car on my word. You are to walk thirty paces straight ahead to the bridge, place the bag on the ground, turn around, and return to your car without looking back. You are to drive away without looking back. Remembering this route will be useless to you. Be advised that you are being tracked by men with automatic weapons. Non-reflective gear, sight-shields and baffled muzzles. You will not be able to see these men using night vision equipment. Step out of the car now."

It did not sound like some grubby gangster playing snatch-and-grab. This sounded more like excellent strategy, or maybe a simple playbook of what worked, per brutal experience in the game. Carl's glance to Barney said perhaps they were in far deeper than their competence.

"What about my wife?" Carl said to the caller.

"Your wife is about to lose another finger if you do not step out of the car now." Click—that was all.

"We don't even know she's alive," said Barney. "We can about-face and burn ass out of here in this tank, right now, and they can shoot all they want."

"No," said Carl, opening the passenger door. "I've got to do this. If somebody nails me, at least…wing 'em, or something."

"I've got your back."

Carl stepped out, exposed, elaborately demonstrating that he carried nothing except the bag, then began to plod toward the bridge. The smell outside was unique, almost physical in its oppressiveness. Barney could see through the binocs that Carl was actually counting his paces.

Non-reflective gear, sight-shields and baffled muzzles. This was big time.

Carl must have sweated off half a pound for every step, to and from. No commotion from the outlands. No snipers in the trees, so far. Not that trees could survive here. He made it back to the limo with all his skin intact, and the phone rang again.

"I see three men coming down for the bag," said Barney. Three shadows, from different directions, vectoring on a target.

"Carl?" The voice on the phone belonged to Erica.

"Baby…?" Carl sounded lost, or damned. His voice had constricted.

Erica was gulping air, sobbing on the other end of the call. "He told me…they told me I have to tell you…"

Barney leaned over to listen, trying to keep an eye on the bag.

"Just say it, baby, whatever it is." Carl was jittering, on the verge of implosion.

"They say you broke the rules," Erica said, parroting what a deep male voice was telling her to say. "You contacted someone. Brought someone with you. That's …that's not allowed. He says…*they* say the ransom is now two million, and this is a down payment." More instruction, then she reluctantly added, "In good…faith that you will not betray them again."

Carl was shouting Erica's name into a dead line.

"No good," said Barney. "We're blown. They'll dump the bag unless we give them a reason to run with it."

Barney floored the accelerator of the limo, heading straight for the bridge.

The night came alive with auto weapons fire.

"*What the hell are you doing—*" Carl hollered.

"Shut up. Get in the back. Head down."

Lacquer chips jumped from the hood of the Town Car as a fusillade of nine-millimeter slugs flattened into the windshield, making starbursts, rude impact hits without the attendant cacophony of gunfire. The voice had spoken true—silencers.

Triangulating, Barney figured four shooters, three of them the guys after the bag. One grabbed and they all scattered two seconds before the limo came to a dust-choked halt near the natural stone foundation.

Barney already had the Army .45 in his hand.

As the car stopped he chocked his door open with his foot and stayed low, popping two rounds and dropping the runner with the bag, who was not shooting. The bag was scooped by another runner who fired back—Uzis, from the sound and cycle rate. Barney

ducked the incoming angry metal bees, mostly discharged unaimed, panic fire, gangsta showoff.

The brake was up and the limo began a slow roll
toward the bridge. This was intentional. Barney crabwalked alongside, scanning around for the bonus
shooter, who expectedly rose from the crest of the
bridge and began shooting downward, ineffectually.
Barney put a triple-tap in his general direction to keep
him down, under cover.

The right front wheel stopped against the outstretched leg of the first guy to grab the bag.

"Now," Barney shouted at Carl. "Drag that sonofabitch in here!"

He spent his final five rounds keeping Bridge Guy
down. It took Carl about five seconds to find his own
spine, then jack-in-the-box out the starboard side of
the limo to collect their captive. Only about one in
twenty fired shots from the darkness was even hitting
the car now. They were back in the thick of battle, and
dormant reflexes and instincts resurged. Carl even
remembered to grab the insensate man's gun, and
hefted it across the seat to Barney just as Barney's clip
ran dry and the action of the .45 locked back.

Barney's hands knew the weapon, a Heckler-Koch
MP5 with a retractable buttstock. A Navy version of
the assault gun favored by SWAT teams, notorious for
having a dicey thumb safety. Barney quickly checked
the cocking handle and then emptied the 30-round
mag at the top of the bridge before he ducked back
into the limo. The integral silencer was starting to
cook already, and the gun was hot as a barbeque.

Sporadic incoming fire tried to hector them, but
their armor was as good as advertised. Barney stomped

the limo into reverse, humping the big vehicle inelegantly out the way they had come.

Carl shouted something about Barney being out of his mind, what was he thinking, they were all sunk now—clear the table, bring in fresh meat and stick a fork in them, because they were *done*.

"Just clock that maggot if he wakes up," said Barney, meaning their guest.

"*What're we gonna do?*" Carl moaned.

"I hate to put it this way, old buddy, but if Erica is still alive, they'll call you, you bet. If they don't call, she's already gone. But if they do call, you tell them that now we've got a hostage, too."

What had just happened?

Past the insanity, when the shouting had abated, what had been accomplished, and why?

That was what Carl would want to know. Barney was stone-faced and silent as he put distance between them and the bad guys, one eye already on the GPS tracker in the limousine. The onscreen map was shifting, stuttering southwesterly—away from them. Carl would want to talk, to quell his rampant panic with chatter; Barney would tell him to please be quiet.

Gunfire produces a surreal, accelerated state of mind, and the first rule is not to be seduced or distracted by the hyper-reality of metal projectiles whizzing through the air all around you, the noise, the muzzle flashes, ricochets and panicked confusion. You must envelop yourself in a pocket of calm deliberation that permits maximal safe evasion, target tracking, and optimum—not wasteful—return fire in order to neutralize the opponent's capacity to kill you. The learned behaviors of firing scared, firing blind, or firing wounded cannot be acquired by advice or instruction; either you got it or you ain't.

The people who had abducted Erica Ledbetter were businessmen in a cruel trade who no doubt thought of what they did as a brutal necessity in a harsh and unforgiving world. If they were good at what they did, they would not gratuitously sacrifice a revenue asset—Erica—for the sake of a macho gesture.

But. But this was Mexico, birthing crib of cowboy machismo. What if their dicks had been scuffed enough to warrant a violent display and alpha-male retribution?

But. But the voice on the cellphone hadn't sounded like a street thug. He'd sounded like a businessman—with an education, which made his status in the kidnapping trade extra-lethal, because here was a person who would not bluff.

But. But Carl and Barney now possessed a counter-hostage, one of the bad guys, currently dozing in the back of the limo after being knocked unconscious by Barney's second shot, a deflection hit that had skinned the hair off his left temple and put his nasty self down into dreamland. Barney's first shot had hit the guy in the ass, and the slug was buried deep in the meat of his right buttock. That would be painful soon enough, and very useful.

But. But Carl would believe Barney was a loose cannon, a gold-card-carrying member in good standing of Club Psycho, for taking provocative action. Carl might not understand that had been the only option. They could accede like sheep or push the ante. The deciding factor for Barney had really been the bullet-proof car. The armored limo had been better than having five extra guys on their side. The Rio Satanas drop-off stank in more important ways than its eye-watering odorama: At the moment Barney had seen the setup, he'd known the drama was far from over, but there'd been no time to explain that to his compadre.

The kidnappers had never wanted an exchange at Rio Satanas, Erica for the cash. They had wanted an excuse to sweeten the pot. They had already known Barney was in play before he and Carl left their seedy hotel, so credit Estrella for sinking them even before they got to the river; Erica was probably miles away. Carl was to be told his desperate gambit—using Barney—had been hopeless. There was to be the requisite gunfire and shouted ultimata. It was designed to play that way so Carl, now more freaked out than ever, would eagerly agree to any solution, any carrot the bad guys offered, like doubling the ransom. Minimal effort, and the kidnappers win two-to-one.

Which was why the only option had been to jab them, see who flinched, maybe score a drop of blood in payback. It had all happened very quickly, and the exchange seemed to have soldiered Carl up. He had dropped back into combat mode, heeding the incoming fire, grabbing their hostage, tossing Barney the MP5, not pointing the muzzle at Barney or himself.

Maybe that was why Carl was being unaccountably quiet right now.

Barney's own return to combat mode had come much earlier. It had surged back instantaneously like a good cocaine bump to his bloodstream. It was all foregone the moment he saw the bridge. Flooring that pedal was as natural for Barney as hitting the brake would be for an ordinary human with a toddler in their path. You either got it or you ain't, and Barney owned it.

He could feel his heartbeat. He was *awake* now, and that was why he had engaged superior forces while hopelessly outnumbered.

Now all he had to do was figure out a way to tell Carl that his saucy little friend Estrella was working for the bad guys.

"He's awake," Carl said from the back of the car.

"The bag has stopped," Barney said, watching the GPS screen.

Barney heard the sound of Carl punching their captive in the face, more than once, sort of as punctuation as he spit invective. It was not necessary, in fact, it was badly advised, but Carl needed a place to put his rage and the impotence of the past few days. You vent the rage, you get it out of yourself, then you can assess more clearly. The downside of shedding your rage is usually that somebody else has to absorb the burden, in this case, one tooth-loosening knuckleblow at a time.

"Hey! *¿Como se llama, puto? ¡Digame, pinche cabron! ¡Repuestame!*"

Thud. Thud.

Hurting them first generally got answers more briskly than asking them first, then hurting them. It was the same as the kidnapping theory: *Pay us or we'll kidnap your wife* would not work nearly as well as the other way around.

"*¡Oigame, pendejo!*" Thud.

"I didn't know you knew so much Spanish," said Barney.

"What about the goddamned bag?" Thud.

"Driving toward it now."

"*¡Nombre, joto!*" Thud, thud.

Their guest tried to respond, in a spray of tooth chips, flecks of blood and bits of his tongue, but Carl was enjoying hitting him too much. Apparently the fellow's name was Jesús.

"*¡Me llamo Jesús, Jesús, chinga tu madre, Jesús! ¡No molestarme!*"

"*¿Se hábla Inglés?*" Carl cocked but didn't strike, and it got the desired response.

"*Sí, un poquito,*" said Jesús, quickly recognizing a wonderful opportunity not to be hit again. "I speak a little. Please, *por favor*, no—" He had his hands up, defensively.

"The guy's just a bagman, Carl; lighten up," said Barney.

"He shot at us."

Point, Barney thought.

"Better start a conversation with my amigo back there," said Barney. "He might keep punching until he breaks on through to the other side."

"*...me cago en la tapa del organo y me revuelco encima de la mierda,*" Jesús muttered.

"What was that?" said Barney.

"Ole Jesús here thinks his world just turned to shit," said Carl, pulling back for a definitive haymaker that caused Jesús to start talking faster.

"Those guys! The guys!" he said. "They just hire me! Pay me to do job!"

"Bullshit, Jesús—you haven't got any *dinero* on you. If they agreed to pay you and you don't have any money, that means you're going to see them again."

"They kill me super-bad if..."

"*I'll* kill you super-bad right fucking now, Zorro!" Carl was not screwing around. The whites of his eyes had pinked in anger, Barney saw in the rearview.

They circled wide and caught up with the bag where it had been dumped, about five miles from the bridge. At least it proved Barney's little GPS trick could work, and gave them a general direction they could employ to strike some good, clean Catholic fear into Jesús.

"Nobody has called," said Carl.

"They're going to sweat you," said Barney.

"*Sí, es verdad,*" said Jesús. "They make you wait."

"So what do we do?" said Carl.

"We clear out of the hotel," said Barney, "because we're all the way made. If Jesús' homing skills don't improve, we're going to have to kill him all the way dead. *¿Comprende?*"

"*Claro,*" said Jesús.

Somebody had already visited the hotel room. Barney had expected that. What came as a shock was what their nocturnal visitors had left behind.

Estrella was completely naked, duct-taped to a tubular metal chair, her neck opened ear-to-ear with a razor. About a gallon of blood saturated the note that had been left nailed into her chest.

> *Rescate = $2M ahora*
> *We Do This to Bitch*

Estrella's eyes were wide-open, unseeing. She had gotten her party, all the way, with no pestersome hangover.

"Hustle," said Barney. "Cops are probably on their way."

The limo was riddled with dents where bullets had hit but they had no time for anything fancier. Once they were back on the road, they looked for someplace they could base themselves with a simple cash payment and no annoying questions. Their gear was piled in the back of the limo since Jesús occupied the trunk. Barney had estimated Jesús was in no danger of bleeding to death; in fact, the wounded bagman told them freely that he had been shot before, that they shouldn't worry about *that*.

What they found was a downscale sex motel called La Pantera Roja, complete with a gated courtyard (to discourage private investigations), individual garages with roll-down doors (so your spouse could not spy your car in the lot), and even a bizarre kind of room service—microwaved pizza or a limited beverage menu could be discreetly delivered to your room via a little revolving airlock-style compartment, like the door on a darkroom. In case the occupants were naked, identifiable, or otherwise tied up.

The headboard of the whorehouse bed was screwed to the wall. The lamps were bolted to the tables. Everything was garishly overpainted. The TV was coin-fed and locked down. A metal band secured the top of the toilet to the tank so nobody would steal it. A payphone was mounted to the brick wall. It was perfect. They were able to drag Jesús inside under complete cover.

"We've got to get some more shirts," Barney said as he rustled the gun cleaning kit in his rucksack to one side to retrieve a roll of duct tape, for Jesús, from whom Carl had also liberated an extra mag of ammo for the MP5.

Jesús was glazed, eyes dilated and breathing shallowly.

Carl could do little apart from watchdogging the damned cellphone, trying to will it to ring.

So Barney was stuck trying to obtain some fresh clothes, minimal food, and another terrific plan. When he returned, the bloodless expression on Carl's face told him that he'd been on the phone.

"Thirty seconds, maybe less," he said, frittering with his hands. "Erica talking, again. Telling me what they told her to. She's alive. At least she was—" he checked his watch "—eight minutes ago."

"They're not going to kill her," said Barney, handing Carl a beer. "What did they say?"

"The usual gangster movie crap about paying the penalty for violating their goddamned rules. Estrella was to demonstrate they are serious. They don't give a damn about ole Jesús, over there. All they want is for me to call them when I get the money. The extra money." Carl killed the beer in a swallow.

Barney quickly checked to see if Jesús had overheard. Nobody home. He was almost snoring, palate clicking, not so much asleep as unconscious.

"You should have heard her, man," said Carl, voice cracking. "Repeating that crap. *Tardiness in any form will result in additional damage to your merchandise.*' Christ."

"I bet they said come unarmed, come alone?"

Carl made a little thumb-and-forefinger gun. "You got it."

"Carl, this guy you know in New York, the money guy. Would you call him a friend?"

"Sure, I guess so. I mean, a million bucks…"

"That's not what I mean. I'm talking about a friend— do you trust him?"

"He's the only person I called before I called you. When I realized this was too deep for me to do by myself. Yeah, he's into all kinds of shady crap, but he's a friend."

"Sort of like me, then," Barney said. "Call when cornered?"

"I guess," Carl repeated, not sure of where this was going.

"But…after you get your wife back, and you go back to your nice, safe American way of living, you still have to find some way to get this guy his money back, right?"

"Sure, I mean…of course." He still looked puzzled.

"How you going to do that, Carl? How're you going to pay the guy back a million bucks? Or two million?"

"I don't know. Barter counts for a lot. He needs people to run straw accounts, dummy corporation drops, money laundering, that sort of thing. He wants me to do something like that, well, I owe him, don't I?"

Barney wondered just how far Carl's ethics permitted the notion of debt. Not money, but actual obligation.

"What's his name?"

Carl looked at Barney as though he had just sprouted eyes on stalks. "I can't tell you that, man."

"Sure you can. These dinks just tried to frame us for a murder, just to make a point. We haven't actually killed anyone yet, but not for lack of trying, plus we kidnapped Jesús there. We're driving around Mexico in a bullet-riddled car with Federales looking for us. You can damned well tell me who your sugar daddy is, your friend, or we are less than friends and I quit—do you copy?"

"For god's sake, it's Felix, all right? Felix Rainer,

in New York. Okay? Happy now? God, what's *with* you?"

Carl would have to phone New York like a deadbeat college kid begging more cash, and Barney hated his reflex desire to listen in on that call, because it meant that Carl's fidelity was sliding into a gray zone. To distract himself from the relentless logic chain forming in his mind, he said, "Want to hear our Plan B?"

"Shoot."

He lowered his voice. "We tag our pal Jesús with the GPS chip and dump him at the nearest clinic. With luck…"

"He'll burn ass back to his bosses." Carl smiled.

"But," said Barney. "You're going to call Felix and get the cash. Because we cannot afford to fake it, not now. Not after gunfire."

Carl's brow furrowed. "We might not even *need* the cash."

Barney forced a smile and it felt like his face was cracking. "What's the matter, Carl? Don't you trust me?" He'd meant it to play as a joke, but it just wasn't very funny.

Why did you come down here? Barney thought to himself as he jacked the car. It was a five-year old BMW M3 with a manual shift, thoroughly alarmed but nothing a Swiss Army knife could not neutralize. Tacking on plates boosted from a junker felt strangely nostalgic, a flashback of bandit thrill from high school, before Iraq, before Carl. No problem: Over a hundred cars were stolen in Mexico City every day. Even the jackers had quotas.

Why did you come down here, really?

It went beyond his talent for fixing problems, being the guy who knew the *how* of things. Scoping the worst possible scenario, then whupping it anyway. The gunfire had brought his adrenaline back, restored the beat to his heart. But what had he gained?

Doubts about Carl Ledbetter, for one thing. Slowly coalescing suspicions about the man presenting himself as a friend.

Like the suspicion that Carl knew the kidnappers, maybe.

Like the premonition that things were about to go rotten if Barney did not stay sharp.

And you know how that nag works, like a toothache, a cold sore, a hangnail that commands far more attention than it merits.

The BMW gave up all its secrets to Barney's touch.

The phone call had been almost comical, like one guy asking another to borrow a DVD. *Another mil? Sure thing, Carl old yeoman, anything for a buddy. Hope it all works out, dude. Later!*

So before Carl embarked to a bank to collect wired funds, Barney had tagged him, not Jesús, with the GPS chip. He had amputated the receiver from what was left of the rental limousine and had it with him as he boosted the BMW, his "job" while Carl was presumably working high finance and Jesús was cooling his wheels and deliriously considering his severely limited options back at the Pantera Roja.

In fractured Spanglish Jesús had requested the bible from the bedside drawer. Barney left the book in his lap so he could thumb the tissue-thin pages with his wrists permanently duct-taped to the metal. Jesús said *gracias señor* to the man who had shot him, squirming uncomfortably on the bullet still lodged deep in his beefy ass. It had to feel like sitting on a flaming poker.

And now Carl was on the move. Not at the bank, not at the motel. In a cab, most likely, and his trajectory was eating up new ground, northeast, into the thick of the city.

Barney hated what he was doing, and did it anyway. That was his special talent, his social mutation, if you will. He recalled more words of the Old Assassin: *"I have no one, I care for no one, and I am cared for by no one. So all I have is what I can do."* Barney disliked feeling beholden, and appreciated that throughout his existence he had taken pains and occasionally made grand, operatic gestures to ensure he never belonged to anyone. He never had.

Except his veneration of the Old Assassin's counsel had obligated him to the memory of the Old Assassin. Great—he kept the guy alive in his head, like one of those shoulder-perching angel-or-devil advisors of conscience, and thus Barney *was* obligated, dammit to hell, connected to someone who had long since chewed that mouthful of grave dirt that awaits us all.

This is not to say Barney did not form liaisons or forge friendships, but there was always a clear demarcation, an unspoken line of hazard tape that could never be crossed, that kept his plus-minus columns internally ordered. He had acquaintances. He had connections. He had friends, but no intimates. He enjoyed the company of women, but no intimacy. He had sex; he had never made love. "Making love" denoted the manufacture of something that would need to be maintained. Barney's golden rule was to always be ready to jump out of the chopper and start shooting at a millisecond's notice. He had never cohabitated with anyone. The closest he ever came was stuff like sharing bedsprung motel rooms with guys like Carl.

Carl, who had now birthed a goblin of doubt in Barney's calm.

There were other people Barney trusted in his limited fashion. Armand, for example, back in the States, feeding Barney's goldfish, which did not have a name other than "the fish." Armand was a champion target shooter fond of the customized assemblies known as "race guns" in the trade. Their relationship was one of mutual gunslinger respect, and they did not pry into each other's biz. There were a few others: Karlov, an old-school gunsmith; Sirius, a jolly ex-cop who was fun to drink with. Most everybody else was take-or-leave as needed; sketches, not people. Background extras. To shut out the noise of their lives was to assist Barney's lifelong quest for a kind of technical purity.

The women he remembered as shades, reduced to one-liners: Jessica, long burnished hair and long of leg, a coffeehouse songstress. Kyrie, another ex-cop, tough as a cement nail. Brianne, his bombshell, too perceptive and destined to be damaged by the world, thus fostering dangerous notions of protection. Geneva, sharp and too smart for him, with centuries of turbulence in her mixed mocha bloodlines. Kate, who pulled him out of his shell long enough to teach him how to dress and otherwise fake human function in public. The Other Kate, who had fooled herself into believing she loved him. Whenever he felt the tendrils of another human being's needs begin to form a chrysalis around him, Barney reversed polarity and repelled them, concentrating on how to simplify his life. Whatever was supposed to emerge from that chrysalis would never be. Barney contented himself with becoming the best possible caterpillar, because it was hard, not convenient, not easy, and therefore not a path most ordinary people would willingly choose. The most rewarding personal effort is always the most difficult.

Such mandarin focus might constrict most lives, which was perhaps another reason Barney had taken on Carl's wild-card proposition. Or maybe it was the arrogance of ego—Barney to the rescue. Maybe it was because he had wired his body for momentum, and stasis could drive him buggy, stir-crazy inside the safe walls of his world.

Whatever the reason or rationalization, Barney would not quit. He was committed to the tactical clarity of eradicating mystery—perfectly in character, for him— and answering these new and unbidden questions, especially the ones he was now asking himself.

Cocooned in his stolen, air-conditioned car, in the company of his guns and jerry-rigged equipment, Barney tailed Carl into an even worse part of town.

Driving in Mexico City is not recommended for the inexperienced (or for that matter, anyone without a death wish), but for Barney it was no worse than, say, Beirut.

The brown brick building had no title. No address. Heavily barred windows; sepia shades drawn. Welded plate steel over the ground-floor ingresses. It looked vaguely industrial, like a sweatshop or piece-goods mill, or the self-contained microcosmic hives where indentured laborers fabricated merchandise for American deep-discount chains. It was three stories tall and

Barney noted that fire escapes had been removed
from the exterior. It was a lost structure amid the
chaos surrounding it—obvious whorehouses, night
spots with glowering security thugs, rave space and
drinking dens, the traffic mortared to gridlock by sidewalk commerce, tented night-market stalls hawking
everything from bootleg DVDs to brown heroin
(abundant and cheap), assorted losers unconscious or
dead in gutters and door archways, viper-mean street
denizens cruising for meat, disenfranchised lunatics
pinballing about, religious pamphleteers, more bored
cops, everybody jostling everybody else in that cultural
denial of personal space that is peculiarly Mexican. The
people here seethed. Here you could smell the food,
the flavors, the populace, the perfume of the city. It
was nasty, exhilarating and more than a little bit lethal.

Carl unfolded himself from the back of one of the
city's omnipresent green-and-white classic VW Beetle
cabs called *vochos*—the kind not advised for tourists
due to the ebb-and-flow trend of robbery, yet cheaper
than hotel-assigned taxis and perfect for anonymity on
the go. He had a big satchel with him, the type of
briefcase used to carry bulky files, with a fold-over
latched top. If that satchel contained money, then Carl
had to be packing at least one firearm, meaning he had
stepped out of character as soon as he thought himself
unobserved. He moved to an iron door, was eyeballed
via a peephole, and was admitted to the murk of the
nameless brown building.

Dusty street brats banged on Barney's window,
trying to sell him chewing gum—known brand names
with slightly modified ingredients best left unspecified. The BMW was an advantage in this 'hood; locals

would assume it was just another drug exec making rounds or extorting protection, but it would also attract urchins and beggars, first the Artful Dodgers, then the kids huffing paint or zoned out on crystal meth. Barney kept his window up and his focus on the building. Some of the kids thumped the car but it was just a show of bravado, a test to get a rise out of the gringo. No sale.

Some people were worth a million bucks. Some were not worth spare change, like Estrella, who had probably been plucked from a stable of a dozen just like her and aimed at Carl with the surety of a cruise missile. She had been butchered for no more than dramatic impact. Point: If Carl only had some back-alley deal cooking, nobody would have bothered to lay Estrella out in a bloody-rare buffet back at their first lodging house. If nothing else, it proved the opposite side was deadly serious.

On the hit list of Mexico's most profligate crimes, kidnapping came third after theft and homicide, and was considered more serious than drug trafficking. In theory the act carried a 30- to 50-year prison sentence. Mexico City accounted for more than half the abductions in the entire country, with the death ratio of victims actually murdered about one in ten. It became so dire that in 2004 a quarter-million citizens protested in Zocalo Square, where the sinking Basilica was located. They called for political reform, they decried police corruption, they called out for implementation of the death penalty. The following year, Mexico City was reported to have the highest kidnapping rate in the world…and the highest percentage of money paid to kidnappers.

So much for Rudy Giuliani and zero tolerance, thought Barney. Giuliani had collected over four million dollars for his consultancy on how to clean up Ciudad Mexico, a place one does not, *cannot*, "clean up."

In the interests of public service, someone conducted a study that reached the prim conclusion that four percent of the kidnappers down here were cops. The real percentage they did not dare suspect out loud.

It was a growth industry in more ways than one. Five thousand separate personal security firms in Mexico City easily billed over a billion dollars per year.

The middle class had imprisoned itself inside walled compounds, requiring bars, latches, locks, codes, dogs, cameras, and beefy enforcers to run it all. It was not unfair, and certainly not gratuitous, to call Mexico City a completely paranoid freefire zone most of the time.

But the contradictions waited to hard-slap you at every turn. You could encounter the kind of aching beauty only noticeable when contrasted with eye-watering squalor. Small kindnesses loomed much larger here. Love was amplified as much as hate, and could broadside unsuspecting outsiders just as completely. There was more dignity in a wizened old man plying a watchmaker's trade in a hole-in-the-wall shop than in all the ostentatious skyscrapers in the richer districts. Folks living in borderline poverty were more honestly generous than their supposed betters. More honor among common people, because to them the lessons had come gruelingly hard. Heads you live and tails you die, and Mexico City was the edge of the coin.

You could fall in love or become a killer, no preamble. And fall back just as quickly. It all depended on how the coin fell, and the coin was forever in mid-air. In lesser men this might be a source of nerve-wracking stress.

To Barney, it was other people's noise, and he could click it all off, could wait with an almost conscienceless patience.

Carl emerged from the fortress building with fresh sweat on his temples. His gaze swept the street, and his manner was the manner of a man who was certainly guilty of…something. He started physically when the BMW skidded up beside him and he found himself staring down the bore of Barney's .45.

"Get in the car," said Barney. "Right fucking now. Not a word."

At least thirty people saw Carl climb meekly into the car at gunpoint. It did not matter to any of them, and was forgotten even before the dust of departure had settled.

"I almost called you on the cell," said Barney. "That might have been a nice little surprise. But it might have gotten you in trouble."

"Thank god you didn't," Carl said, practically mumbling.

The gun was stowed. It had made its point, and its threat was implicit.

"You want to tell me what the hell is really going on?"

"I don't know what you're—"

"*Don't*. Do. That." Barney's tone was as serious as a nuclear core meltdown. "I want to know what you've mixed me up in, and what you have to do with it. Not the story. The truth. Start anytime, because I'll keep your ass in this car for a week until you come clean."

Carl fumbled, hands uselessly grasping the air before him, trying to twist nothing into some sensible shape.

"Start with your drop-off at the building back there."

Still nothing. Where to begin?

"All right, try something simpler. What's your cut?"

Any pretense to standing fast collapsed, as though Carl's face had been unscrewed. "Half." He spluttered. "Look, it ain't broken...I can fix this. I can pay you. I was going to pay you anyway. A lot. More than your trouble, because you came to help me. I can pay you—"

Barney pulled the pistol back into sight to shut him up. "What I want, old buddy, cannot be paid in dollars or pesos or doubloons. You are a world-class fuckup, Carl. You got yourself conned into a scam too big for you, and it could still backfire and blow your dick off. Worse, you involved your wife, and even worse, you took advantage of a friend. It's long past the time to shrug and go *oh well*. Frankly, I'm not amazed you're that gullible. I am amazed that you'd come up with such a cowboy idea and throw your wife into the pot."

"That's why I have to tell you about Erica," Carl said. Contritely. "It was her idea."

Carl had saved Erica (so he related) from a stalker boyfriend with a history of vague threats and backhanded harassment. She would get flooded with junk mail based on credit card offers or find her parked car keyed, but nothing ever tracked back to the ex, one Rafe Torgeson. By Erica's account, Rafe had been one of those sexy, seems-like-a-good-idea-at-the-time diversions who become dysfunctionally possessive/

obsessive once they graduate from cheap thrills to what desperate people call a "relationship"…once they start clinging, fighting more than fucking, struggling for air, slamming down ultimata and grabbing for some kind of illusory life preserver that was never there to save them in the first place.

By Erica's account.

And if you're Erica, who can you get to believe your account? No one who's known you long enough to see you go through this cycle before. No one at all — unless, of course, you meet someone new, with whom you have no history, who will believe virtually anything you tell them. Clean slate. Refreshed story to tell. Modify as you go.

Erica was the sort of woman, said Carl, who refused to believe she was not important enough for everyone to obsess over. She needed a history of epic betrayals and close calls in order to curry her next host, like any decent parasite. To say she was a drama queen was to undervalue her wiles. She was not interested in hot gossip so much as fundamental blackmail material.

Picture it: *God, Carl, I don't know where to turn, this guy has made my life a living hell, I'm not asking you to save me, just let me stay the night.* Great in a movie, awful in real life because it reminds you of the real meaning of awe. All that is needed is a few pheromones, an auto-response sense of protectiveness for those of whom you have grown fond, and time for the whole stew to rot.

Carl had come to realize that the epically evil Rafe Torgeson, along with most of the other disaster exes cited by Erica, were her idea of confections. There was not a shred of actual proof of any of the thousands of crimes against poor, innocent Erica, who only wanted to help people…with the exception of her victims, like Rafe Torgeson and whomever else was back-dated on her dance card.

Carl logically concluded that sooner or later, he would become the next evil ex, just as soon as Erica had adequately prepped a fresh host full of new, unpolluted blood. Every disagreement, every conflict, every suggestion of hers not scooped up with a military sense of command, was another notch off Carl's clock.

Erica, in turn, had smelled that her latest host had passed his spoilage date early, and to demonstrate her skill at manipulation she preemptively proposed the Plan.

Then she screwed Carl's brains to mush, just to show there were no hard feelings. Predators never hang onto to devalued marks, and prefer quick exits, except in the case of vendetta, where they opt for the slow, lingering demise—gangrene instead of amputation.

"I knew I was outplayed," said Carl. Anonymous streets whizzed past the closed windows of the BMW. "But damn it, I still loved her, or thought I did. You know? She came along right when I had decided not to cut and run from relationships so easily. I had decided to work at the next one…and she came along as the next one. I was ripe and she could smell it."

"That's really touching," said Barney. "I assume you have a point floating around in all that self-pity."

"The Plan. Erica knew about Felix Rainer, in New York. I had confided enough to her for her to know that Felix was a financial exposé waiting to happen. How much do you know about the Mexican economy?"

"I'm getting impatient, Carl, goddammit."

"No, wait!" Carl locked eyes with Barney. "It's relevant and it's the truth. Please."

Barney waited.

"Do you have any idea what a hot pot it is down here? More journalists are gunned down in Latin America than in Iraq, man! There are fourteen hundred municipalities down here that don't even have access to banks—that's how backward things are. Meanwhile the United States is getting ready to exploit eighty percent of Mexico's natural gas resources —and do you know what they're paying with? Water. Access to water. Water from the United States, which also buys four-fifths of the petroleum here, and it's all owned by two companies, Petroleos and Pemex, and guess who owns *them*? And it's not just oil. It's trucking contracts, guys buying tanker ships, drivers, loaders, storage, all of it heading for America, baby. Along with stuff like genetically contaminated corn, for which the environmental reports were shoveled under; poultry and processed eggs with phytosanitary problems, pesticide-infected cherries—all of which winds up as your chicken Caesar or in your Manhattan. A dozen wars are going on, between Mexican sugar and American fructose, between milk companies in Coahuila and Jalisco. Beer distribution here has been taken over by Heineken and Coors, and they paid over a billion dollars for the privilege: Tecate, Dos Equis, Carta Blanca and Bohemia—even the Sol we've been drinking. Yet guerillas blew up seven oil and natural gas pipelines last week; that's hundreds of millions in lost production. The whole system down here is caving in on a daily basis. It's Wild Wild West time for opportunists, and that's where Felix Rainer's dirty money comes into the picture."

If Carl had been looking for an opportunity to unburden himself, he had definitely been pacing and rehearsing.

"When cellphones liberated common people—when they allowed people who had never *seen* phones to *have* phones, just like in China—the telecommunications companies flooded Latin America with networking technology. Down here, people kidnap each other for ransom. Up there, in the rarified air, executives are cutting each other's throats over satellite placement but it's just as gruesome. And every single company suffers skyrocketing costs, due to guess what? Security. The paranoia that keeps security a big issue is important, because that, too, translates as money."

"Cellphones?" What the fuck was Carl talking about? This was not just babble to buy time, or misdirection. Carl sounded as though he was honestly losing his mind. "You need to start making some sense. Now."

"Listen. Illegal systems hijack billions of call minutes per year. That's just one of the ways Felix collects his pennies. And no matter how many Cayman Islands accounts you try to hide, the Feds will notice a huge pile of money sooner or later, and you've got to move it around. If you can't launder all of it, you redistribute it."

"So the ransom Felix supplied you with goes to the kidnappers, who aren't really kidnappers, and trickles through into dozens of ancillary business interests down here, legal, illegal and 'other.' "

"I'm not sure exactly how. I don't know all the details. But the kidnappers are real. They have to be real."

"Or no one will buy the kidnapping?"

"Nobody cares about little meat-market hostages. But if it is big-ticket enough, it's going to attract businessmen the same as the drug trade. So, point two: the score has to be big."

"Two million big."

"And that's just one grab. Felix knew a corrupt Captain in the Judicial Police down here, and made a few calls, and then a few trips."

Barney could smell rotting strawberries, or maybe rotting psyche. The stench of gone-over bouquets in rancid gray water.

"So they set up high-priced kidnappings," Barney said, "and Felix is able to transfer money from his legitimate accounts to 'save' his amigos—probably under a variety of names—and that frees up shelf space for his less-legitimate money?"

"Something like that."

Barney briefly considered resigning from the human race, turning his back on the world, and perhaps leaving civilization for the maggots to consume. No wonder he felt like an isolationist. He tried to shuck off the weight that had settled onto his shoulders. "So how's good old Felix making out with this scam?"

"Way too successful," said Carl. "So successful, in fact, they're thinking of diversifying out of Mexico. Grabbing their hostages in the States and smuggling them down here for ransom."

The gargoyles had really taken over the cathedral. Maybe it wasn't too late to find a red button and nuke the whole planet.

"Is the goddamned kidnapping real or not, Carl?"

"Yes and no."

"Please don't make me start hitting you."

"It has to pass muster as a genuine kidnapping.

Believe it or not, even down here there are police reports, genuine investigations, paper trails. It has to look, smell, act, and shit real. Whole food chains of players who must be convinced. If kidnappers diversify, the guys above them have to believe they haven't gone soft, aren't cheating the system in any way. You can't just pay off everyone to lie. The snatchers have to think they've abducted a real victim. The keepers have to believe they are watchdogging a legitimate hostage. The money men have to believe they are trafficking at the potential cost of a real human life."

"I can just keep driving north until we're at the border," said Barney, hoping his warning was clear as distilled water.

"Yeah, yeah, okay...Erica talked to Felix. Felix talked to me. Then Erica talked to me. We invest three days, a week, tops, and walk away with a million to split, fifty-fifty. We allow Erica to be kidnapped and ransomed. We make it look so real that we get the payout doubled, and nobody on the outside suspects it's anything but crime as usual, what a damned shame. We rescue Erica, but only after the money has changed hands. Bang—everybody's safe, everybody's richer, and Erica goes her own way with her new bank, and I get to go mine."

"Wait a fucking minute," said Barney. "That drop at the bridge. Are you telling me you *knew* those scumbags? They were shooting *live* ammo at me, Carl!"

"No! I...I...didn't know them, personally, I mean. It had to be real. If *you* bought it, as an outside agent, then it would look watertight, and—"

"And you didn't have the balls to do it yourself," Barney overrode.

"You asked me for the truth," said Carl. "I'm trying

to give you that. You don't have to make me feel like a
shit. I'm already doing a great job of that myself. If you
want to punch me out, go ahead. Yell. Shoot me. But
don't give me that child-molester look, like you're not
going to be my best friend at school anymore. I have to
get free. I conned you. I'm sorry, but there you were—
all capability and no connections. Certainly no connections like Erica, who I have to get free of. You see?"

"No, I do. Not. See. Carl."

A gruesome silence settled between them. Carl had
raved. Now he needed to think up something else to
say—anything else to reacquire Barney's sympathy.
Carl was jabbering himself into a hole...

...which should have made the rest brutally clear
and simple for Barney: Abandon Carl. Free Jesús, who
was a blameless gunner needing a hospital and a few
days off. Barney no longer trusted Carl to do that.
Then: Get to the airport. Use another of his stack of
blind credit cards. Leave. No luggage, no souvenirs.
Pitch the gun so its tainted memories would not hang
around. Forget Mexico. Resume being a ghost. As the
Old Assassin had told him: "*Between missions, I cease
to exist.*" Barney would be okay until he found a worthier mission. Or worthier friends.

But what Carl decided to say was the wrong thing.

"It's not personal, man. It's just business."

Barney might have forgiven, though not forgotten,
all of Carl's transgressions if he had not uttered that
last. It was the weaseldick rationale of the serial coward.
It was the free ride clause big money could buy. It was
the price for which your friends sold you out when
they decided to exchange your friendship for a bargain.

"I'm out," said Barney. "I'm already gone. Keep your

money. Clean up your own mess. And after that you are never to speak to me again."

"No, hey—wait, man, we can fix it, I swear!"

"Carl." Barney spoke softly, motioning Carl to lean closer for a confidence. Then he crossed with his left and plowed his fist into Carl's hopeful half-smile, dialing his lights down to dreamland. Carl flopped back against the passenger door with a busted nose and one tooth perched on his shirtfront.

"Shut up," Barney said.

Jesús was gone.

In fact, all traces of Barney and Carl's base of operations at the motel were gone. Fresh linens, squared sheets, the chair back at the desk and the bible back in the drawer, no blood anywhere.

Barney's body pricked to high alert. He pulled out the .45, knowing a slug was already chambered.

"No way he could've gotten out alone. I taped him up myself." He wheeled, murder in his eyes, which were now looking directly at Carl.

Carl actually backed off two paces. One of his front teeth was in his shirt pocket and his face was already swelling from Barney's punch. He stammered, "I don't know what's going on. Not me."

Footsteps. Concealed soldiers breaking cover and rallying.

A lot of men with a lot of guns—street sweepers loaded with devastating shredder rounds, machine guns with mags of fifty-plus—were boxing them in from both sides of the breezeway. Their safeties had never been on.

Barney's eyes quickly sussed the trap. To bolt for

the car would just mean a Chinese fire drill of gunplay. No way to hole up in the room—the bathroom window was heavily barred and these dudes could shoot through the walls until the entire building fell apart. A quick glance at Carl—useless as a hostage, and honestly confused; what was landing on their heads had not been his idea. Barney had been so intent on watching Carl for the slightest new cheat that he had missed the smell of ambush, the hundred little wrong things that could tip you. They were center stage, spotlit, with no odds and no exit strategy.

Barney's arm brought the gun around regardless, to wax the nearest oncoming gunner. Carl's hand arrested its arc.

"Don't," said Carl, not looking at him.

There were at least eight men, all unafraid of wielding big weapons in broad daylight. Their team lead was a huge, vaguely Samoan monster; three hundred pounds (mostly above the belt) with a shaved head, a wooden idol face and the tiny, rapt eyes of a pit viper. His wifebeater tee revealed pale wormbursts of stretch-marks radiating from his armpits to his shoulders—a sure sign, Barney knew, of an overdose of steroids and iron-pumping.

Nobody said a word.

In short order, Barney was divested of his armament. Both he and Carl were professionally frisked. The room was certified as clear—silently, by a guy who wore mirrorshades so thin they appeared to be growing out of his skull instead of perched upon it. Barney and Carl were marched to a waiting panel van, one badboy on each bicep doing the military-style bring-along with a vise-grip like a pit bull. They were seated roughly, heads sacked, hands cuffed, and the van door slammed shut with a crunch of finality.

The inside of the van smelled like all the guns that had been brought to bear. Humid and close. The sack on Barney's head stunk of motor oil and acetone; somebody had used it as an engine rag. B.O. and hair pomade. Of course, somebody farted. Acidic.

Barney heard Carl's muffled voice say, "What *is* this; you guys all *mutes* or somethi—?"

Thud.

Instantly, they were on the move.

Something was coming up, Barney knew. If nothing waited to complicate their situation, they would have been killed on the spot. So somebody wanted something from them. Maybe Jesús, spoiling for a bit of biblical eye-for-an-eye. Maybe the police, going all Gestapo to take them down for the murder of Estrella without any questions. Maybe Carl's unknown handlers, imposing more conditions and specifications. Strictly business, amigo.

Maybe Erica, ready to yank off her human mask and reveal her true, bloodthirsty nonhuman self.

Maybe the concession on lies and made-up stories did not stop with Carl.

Barney's battle mode was cranked full-up. First opportunity, smash faces, shed blood, obtain a weapon. If no weapon was available, use furniture, glass from a window, his own bones, anything. Walk out of Mexico with no water, naked if he had to.

The first step was to get an arm free, snatch an opportunity. Every journey starts with a first step. This one would never get started as long as Barney was cuffed, masked, blind and bulldogged. All he could do was tick off the silent minutes of their portage. No one spoke. Presumably they were communicating, unseen by their cowled captives, with nods, winks, points; implied degradation, predigested visual jokes. The crew that had taken him and Carl were hardcore professionals. A few good men. Shakespeare had said that: *A few, that is eight*.

To Barney, gunners were not as dangerous as bona fide gunmen. These men were gunners, but they were very good at what they did. Maximum threat potential. No slipups allowed.

They were rousted from the van—Barney had no idea whether Carl had regained consciousness or not —and muscled across graveled pavement, through a door, down a narrow hallway. Another door. An elevator.

A chair, secured to the floor. A set of cuffs for each wrist. The chair was metal, immobile.

The sack rasped off Barney's head.

He was in a second- or third-floor room about twelve by twelve, facing a desk with several flat-screen monitors, a multi-line phone system, a bank of cellphone chargers. Little army men on one corner of the desk sorted out their toy battle plan. Painted jungle camo; tiny guns.

The huge Samoan-looking badass stood behind Barney and folded his arms. His weight creaked the floorboards like tectonic plates. Carl was not in the room.

"Who are you?" said a voice—it was the voice Barney had overheard on Carl's hostage cellphone, back at the bridge.

A man rose up from behind the confusion of com-

puter screens. Five-ten, pattern baldness, well manicured, expensive suit, inarguably Mexican but without
a trace of Hispanic accent.

Barney exhaled nasally. This was how it always
started. The pseudo-politeness, following by the punch
in the face for emphasis. He heard the giant behind
him move, cocking back for a flat-handed blow to the
back of the head. He steeled himself.

"No need, Sucio," the man said. "Not just yet."

Barney could smell the big guy's disappointment.

"Let's skip the patty-cake, shall we?" said the man.
"Instead I'll ask, what are you doing here? Why have
you involved yourself?"

"What's the point?" Barney said. "Get on with it."

"Here's your situation," said the man, walking around
to lean on the front of the desk. "For irrelevant reasons, our friend Carl chose to make a contact outside
our explicit circle, which was prohibited. No doubt he
lacked the honor to conclude the deal which he himself
negotiated; no matter—you are now involved. What
do we do with you?" His voice had the same curious
lack of inflection or accent that Barney had noticed
over Carl's cell. "Do we let you free if you promise
never to whisper a word of this to anyone? Unlikely.
Do we manhandle you and hope the damage serves to
insure your silence? No, just look at you. Beating you
up would do us no good although I think Sucio would
enjoy aspects of it."

"Carl is a shitbag," said Barney. "He conned me. Do
whatever you want to him and his accomplice wife. I
just want out. I don't care what any of you do. I made
an error in judgment. I'm willing to pay for that however you like. But your operation is not in danger. I
have no stake."

"That sounds very ethical, my friend, but there is still the matter of Sucio's cousin Jesús."

"*Mi hermano*," said the giant behind Barney, with a voice like two cinderblocks grinding together.

"Excuse me, his brother."

"I was going back to the motel to set him free, once I found out about Carl. I'm sorry about the misunderstanding." He noticed that the man, who had never introduced himself, seemed to have one lazy eye. Barney did not look at him directly all that much, but when he did, it was a toss-up as to which eye to follow. Bell's Palsy, perhaps—the left side of his face seemed less active, which might account for the squint.

"It's more than a misunderstanding, my friend. Jesús is dead. He bled to death, reading the bible. This is Mexico. I'm afraid it doesn't look very good for you."

"No one dies from a bullet in the ass."

"Ah. But as I believe an autopsy will confirm, Jesús died from a brain hemorrhage caused by your *other* gunshot. I have a doctor working on that right now."

"He shot at me first."

"Mm. But Carl was not supposed to return fire, nor was he allowed to have anyone with him, much less an expert shot such as yourself."

"I didn't know about Jesús. It was an accident." It was all Barney had.

"You do realize how that sounds?" said the man.

"Yes, but it's the truth. You guys butchered Estrella just to leave a memo; you realize how *that* sounds?"

"Her actual name was Salvación, and she was recruited from a group that does not concern us."

"Who was *she* related to? The other women you find to donate fingers?"

"Again, not your concern."

"Listen—just get Carl and his black widow wife in here and they'll tell you. Obviously you're not going to believe anything I say, so stop playing the movie bad guy and jerking off with your little speeches, okay?" Barney was resigned to whatever beating or retribution was coming; it was the only way of staying level in the face of chaos.

"Unfortunately, that is not possible. Carl and his wife are on their way back to the United States. The proper funds have changed hands and our deal with them is done, which leaves you as a loose end. And there is the matter of Sucio's brother, not to mention the difficulty you have caused by your uninvited involvement. They mentioned—that is, Carl and his wife mentioned—that you might actually have some value as a hostage yourself, that your government may be willing to pay for you. Your military record and so on. We are looking into that. In the meantime, I'm afraid you have no option but to remain here as our guest."

Then Sucio hit him, hard, in the back of the head with what felt like an iron dictionary.

All of the lies Barney had lived by, all his isolationist maxims and misanthropy, his fables of a higher calling, the thin tissue latticework of rationalizations that he was somehow purer, better, more dedicated than ordinary humans, all the rules by which he had ordered his existence, were about to evaporate in the crucible of his pain.

Part Two
The Bleeding Rooms

A lot of grunts in the unit have heard of RICO statutes, but few of them know what the acronym stands for: Racketeer-Influenced and Corrupt Organization, which handily defines most of Iraq's assorted Ministries—the Ministry of Health, of the Interior, Education, Water Resources, Oil, Labor and Social Affairs. The list goes on unto boredom, with each ministry more corrupt than the last. Untouchable by investigators and immune to prosecution thanks to militia support from Shia leaders, each formerly legal enterprise has been overrun by criminals and there is no operative difference between the terms "militia" and "gang." It is like Chicago during the Roaring Twenties, but without the charm, the music, or the tuxedos.

(*At least you had the security of knowing everyone around you was the enemy*, said a small voice in Barney's head.)

The majority of casualties to Barney's unit have been the result of Improvised Explosive Devices—IEDs—which are left lying around with the frequency of litter, waiting for some stupid American in body armor to disturb them. *Boom*, and the guy who gave you a cigarette and lit it for you while sitting across from you in the Humvee ships home with no legs and half his eyesight.

Paranoia is not only rampant in the Sunni Triangle, it is wholly justified. You essentially cannot even go to the head without a buddy watching your six. Patrols are wired tight and your areas of safe movement are strictly limited by arbitrary (and sometimes illusory) boundaries. You shoot hoops with your crew, you have to designate one of them to watch for snipers because you've dared to be outdoors.

Sometimes guys just disappear. No record, no rescue, just sucked off the face of the earth as though they had never existed. The fear level acts as a practical version of the boogeyman.

You are either bored to within an inch of self-mutilation because of no action, or scared to death from too much. No middle ground.

The heat is a living, malignant thing. Even the climate seeks to destroy and demoralize you. You do your job while trying to ignore the sound of your eyeballs pan-frying in your skull, wait for your DEROS, and hope you do not lose any vital parts in between.

Virtually every long stretch of road is nicknamed a "highway of death." The US forces in Iraq face the same problem the Soviets had in Afghanistan—lack of adequate security forces for travel or any kind of troop movement. Whenever a vehicle hits a land mine, eats an IED, or is taken out by an RPG, there is usually an insurgent with a video camera to record the flaming vehicles and dead or dying Americans and deliver it via the Arab TV networks to show the enemy is vulnerable. You need a whole armored division to adequately protect a road, and as long as the troops are there, nothing ever happens.

Until something does.

(Who ordered you to take a nap? said the voice in Barney's head. *Snap to.)*

❖

The mine blows both the starboard wheels off the Humvee in which Barney is riding, and flips it. The driver had tacked to avoid what turned out to be a decoy in the road, a suspicious irregularity designed to make you swerve into a real, better-concealed trap. This happens in the middle of a hellacious sandstorm that has reduced visibility to about three feet. No warning; just the eardrum-imploding crack of a bomb going off beneath your vehicle's chassis armor (which did not function worth a damn because there was not enough of it); you go gravity-less like shorts in a dryer in total silence because you are temporarily deaf, and when you can refocus your eyes, everything is on fire.

Your body armor becomes an impediment, its bulk preventing you from jumping out of the vehicle and getting back to a place where the ground is *down* and the sky is *up*, and as you scramble you notice your feet are aflame.

Later you find your boots partially melted; your feet are burned badly enough to prevent you from humping out on your own power.

No glorious mission, no taking that essential hill, just panic and terror as your team scatters into the merciless, sandblasting wind. Nobody knows who is dead and who is alive. What you first think to be enemy gunfire is the rounds in Sgt. Tewks' magazine exploding from the heat. Tewks takes one in the calf from his own weapon.

Everybody gets immediately lost in the sandstorm and no one can hear anything. Barney scrambles like a mad crab to get distance, and flops on his back from a sudden jolt of pain in his side. A piece of the Humvee is jutting out of him, having breached a seam in the constrictive oven of his body armor. He tries to sleeve sweat from his vision and sees his own blood.

Nothing on earth sounds like an AK-47 on full auto. It makes a kind of chopping racket, hence "chopper," before the slang got updated to mean Hueys. They sound similar to the old Thompsons, but not exactly the same, and Barney knows the difference from experience. Most of the gunfire is Kalishnikovs; very little return fire from the Belgian M249 Minimi SAW his unit is packing, even less of the pop-and-crackle of M4s or M16A4s, the standard field issue. The enemy is pot-shotting them where they lie.

He tries to claw out his sidearm, his carbine already swallowed by blowing sand, which is covering him up like snowfall. All of a sudden it hurts to move. Anything. Any second now a renegade with an AK-47 will spot him, helpless as a turtle, and add a bunch of holes to his life. Time slows to grains of sand, trickling.

A buddy grabs his arm and hauls him to a kneeling position, pointing and shouting the path to rally, to comparative safety.

It is their passenger, their observer for the day, their guest journalist from the States.

It is Carl Ledbetter.

Barney woke up.

They starved Barney for a week to tenderize him, then began messing with him, because they could.

He was not much of a fighter on one Styrofoam cup of water per day.

His pacing circle was eight feet from the thin futon

pad on the floor. They had taken his boots. The cuff
on his leg was eight inches long, impossible to slip,
custom-fabricated, attached to a case-hardened steel
chain through a special double-eyelet. The chain fed
back to a wall inset and looped through a metal U-bolt
secured inside its own little grated cage. Somebody
had done a lot of thinking about prisoners and the
ways they escaped, when given oodles of time and
nothing to do. At either end, the chain bore no lock—
thus, no lock to pick.

His pants had been slit to accommodate the big
shackle. Same pants he had worn before, just grimier.

There was not a single sharp object, potential blud-
geon or metal edge in the entire room. No lamps to be
shattered for parts or glass. Screw and bolt heads had
been welded or sheared smooth. No bathroom except
for a squat toilet in the Thai style, within reach of the
chain radius. Therefore no tank lid, no toilet parts to
adapt as weapons or picks. No daylight, although there
was a barred and locked-down window behind steel
mesh, out of reach of the chain. No night, because the
inset ceiling lights (unreachable and unbreakable)
burned 24/7.

When they gave him food, it was usually something
wrapped in a tortilla. No utensils. No plates. No paper
towels or napkins. No dessert.

No clocks.

Trapped, sweltering, occasionally delusional from
no time-sense and no diurnal/nocturnal shift, it was
easy for Barney to hallucinate, then nightmare. The
parallels to Iraq were too abundant. He had to try to
remember things: Where he was, how he had gotten
here, what had gone wrong, what could be done.

He arbitrarily benchmarked the first day he got
beaten up as Day One, although it could have been
Day Five or Week One; Barney had no idea how long
he had been unconscious after Sucio had smashed in
the back of his head.

On Day One, Sucio and some of the thugs who had
taken Barney at the Pantera Roja formed a circle and
pounded the crap out of him, playing keep-away with
his head. Barney swallowed a lot of his own blood.
They abandoned him when he could not stand up to
even make a pretense of defense.

Barney was down in a dark hole for a long time after
that, and by Day Two, he apprehensively guessed that
he might already have been in this place as long as a
month. It was impossible to tell. His brief sessions of
sleep were frighteningly deep, like coma.

He had to use his noodle, or plummet into insanity,
or worse, despair.

His first breakthrough was the discovery of some
reading matter—a copy of the Mexican tabloid ¡Alarma!
from which the staples had been removed. It was all in
Spanish and was at least five years old. Yellow jour-
nalism at its finest. Some of the lurid photos—auto
wrecks, murders, kidnappings, assorted decapitations
—at least gave Barney visual images on which to center
his attention. That the staples had been extracted from
the fold-over newsprint suggested that the tabloid
might have been left here on purpose, the better for
prisoners to fantasize their most extravagant fates, and
thus foment less trouble.

Barney's second breakthrough was noticing the guy
apparently named Mojica. Barney remembered Mojica,
the little ferret-like sonofabitch with the mirrorshades.

Mojica with the obsessively manicured beard that ran like a gray penciled line delineating his jaw. From Mojica's hair and beard growth, Barney calculated that he had been prisoner no longer than a week.

Mojica, of course, was a cousin of the late Jesús, hired thug and bible student. Mojica got his nasty little punches and kicks in generally after the giant Sucio had done the prep work, the major softening up of the subject—the assaultee.

More unconsciousness.

They roughhoused Barney about once every three meals after they started feeding him; mostly brown mystery paste in a tortilla. Diarrhea rollicked his GI tract. His tormentors never spoke except to laugh or exchange insults with one another, so Barney decided to speak to them:

"Hey, *maricón, ¿donde está mi television?*"

A fat guy named Zefir kicked Barney in the gut and Barney vomited on him.

Past a certain point—pretty quickly, if you have learned how to take a bruising—actual pain becomes a vague true north. Barney knew what he had provoked and had prepared mentally for the onslaught.

For the first time, his jailors regarded him queerly, as though they suddenly did not have the upper hand. That was all the victory Barney sought from that little gambit.

Next up: "Hey, Sucio: *¡Oye, tu madre!*"

No complex insult was needed. Mexican invective was extremely touchy on the subject of anyone's mother, and the blackest curse was always assumed. You did not have to call her a whore or suggest a dirty coupling; all you had to do was say *"madre"* instead of "*mama*" to get your target to blow like a volcano.

Sucio actually punched one of the other guys to get up close and personal with Barney that time. He shoved, then struck, a smaller fellow apparently nicknamed Condorito, who had an unfortunately prevalent Mexican body type: low-slung, bow-legged, no ass to speak of. Condorito went submissive, then beat Barney up third in line.

While he was bludgeoning Barney, Sucio unleashed his idea of a poisonous stream of rancid insult. He went crimson and saliva sprayed. What he failed to realize was that he had violated the hitherto-uncrossed line, and was yelling at Barney directly, thus acknowledging his existence.

When his compatriots pulled Sucio off Barney, Barney recognized another important watershed: They did not want to kill him yet, either right away or accidentally.

Between meals and punching-bag sessions, Barney gathered other useful intelligence.

One of the guys—Zefir—made reference to other rooms with other prisoners, some of which *did* have television sets. Which made the building an operative concern as a hostage hotel, thereby helping Barney define where he was. Some of the legitimate or high-ticket captives apparently interested Zefir, a porcine man fond of making fornicatory gestures with his hands. *¿Chicas, retozonas, panochas, papayas muy bonitas, eh?*

Another had said something about a courtyard inside the building, which implied that while fortressed from the street, an area within the structure was open to sky like an atrium.

A further slip of Condorito's tongue had clarified other "guests" as actual hostages (*rehéns*).

Sucio had appropriated Barney's Army .45 and had waved it in his face on several occasions. Since he kept it shoved into his waistband, the bore smelled like his crotch, which was no treat at all.

Several days passed and while the casual beatings continued, they came with no actual threat or grisly detail of what Barney's eventual fate might be. No ransom, no payoff, nothing. Also no change of clothing, no bath, and no room service. Barney began to feel like a moldering corpse that lacked the sense to know it was dead.

It was important for him to remember the name Felix Rainer, although most days, Barney could not recover enough short-term memory to know why. He repeated the name to himself while bunched into a corner on his filthy sleeping pad, rocking back and forth. Felix Rainer. Carl Ledbetter. And Carl's wife, Erica. Every body-blow was another entry on a past-due bill that was slowly, excruciatingly becoming more expensive.

It was generally a bad sign when one of Barney's jailors showed up alone. Today it was Mojica.

Usually, a solo entrance was the cue for some off-the-books sadism, or at the very least, a harsh kick in the balls laced with tons of spittled obscenities about Barney's *madre*.

"Hey, you. Guy. You awake?"

Barney did not know Mojica could speak, let alone speak passable English. He rolled up from his fetal curl on the floor. Something about his attitude threw out defense warnings on a subdermal level; he could not help that, or prevent or disguise it. It did nothing to dispel the flies intent on eating every drop of his sweat, or the gnats (what he'd heard called "see-nots" in the American South) they kept trying to set up housekeeping in his eyes. He didn't even want to think about what was living in his hair by now. Or infesting his groin, or tape-worming up his anus while he tried to sleep.

"Listen, man, I'm not here to hurt you."

Oh, great, I feel so much more cuddly now.

"Seriously." Mojica chanced a couple of steps nearer. Not quite within grabbing distance, given the chain on Barney's leg.

"Listen. You don't gotta say nothing if you don't want to."

If Barney was sketching an insulting caricature, he would have written that dialogue down as *joo don' godda say notheeng if jew dun wanna.* But that shit had never worked in books, never worked in movies, and rarely worked when you were trying to dehumanize your opponent in order to justify killing him without compunction. Barney decided to respond, to indicate that he still had two dendrites of intelligence not rolling around loose on the floor.

"What do you want, Mojica?"

Mojica smiled as though finding out an injured pet was still alive. "Oh, you awake, eh?"

"Let's get this over with. Your *primo* was an accident. I was going to let him go."

"Nah, it ain't that." He came closer, confidentially. "El Chingon is keeping you here; I don't know why 'cos you're not a hostage, man, you understand what I'm saying?"

"*Entiendo*," said Barney. "*Claro*. Who's El Chingon?" It was a slang term for the bossman, El Mero-Mero, big dealski—literally, as in *el gran chingon: the head fucker*. That would be Mr. Lazy-Eye-Doesn't-Talk-Like-A-Mexican, but his drones probably called him *el jefe*, at least to his face.

"Don't ask me shit I can't tell you."

"Fair enough. So what do you want?"

"I want to show you something." Mojica moved forward with his body, cautiously, looking for a sign that Barney would not attack.

"Mojica, I'm too fucking tired to get into it with you…"

"Here." Mojica popped a can of America's second most popular soft drink and handed it over. "You like this, right?"

Barney regarded the chilled can in his grasp with befuddlement and briefly wondered if it was drugged, then decided it did nōt matter. The first swig burned all the way down, fizzy and caffeinated and shot through with sugar, beautiful carbonated nirvana. In times like these, simple, small things could freight tons of meaning. If you had asked Barney what he wanted most of all the things in the world, in that moment, he might have answered that he already held in his hand all good things, and could die happy.

"Look at this," said Mojica, removing his ever-present mirrorshades. He pointed at a small skidmark of scar tissue on his right temple. "See this?" When he pressed the scar, it went concave, then *boinked* back as though made of rubber. He turned his head to show the lower portion of his right occipital. A similar scar, similarly gelid.

"I got shot in the head once," he said. "Brains came

out, so maybe I'm not the smartest *vato* in the world. But I tell you this—they killed my ass. I was dead once. And I'm still here."

Barney's hand loved that soft drink can; would not give it up. Nor use it to hit Mojica in the side of the skull so hard that what was left of his brains would come flying out his ear. Not until he finished the drink, anyway, because it was too good. Mojica had bought himself an audience for whatever confessional he cared to stage.

"This ain't right, them keeping you," Mojica said. "We grab people, we got all this set-up, we don't torture hostages, and anyway you ain't a hostage."

"You kicked my ass with the others."

"Because I ain't stupid, man. But keeping you here…I mean, for what? So Sucio can whale on you until you're a retard? There ain't no ransom on you. No pickups, no negotiation, *nada por nadie*. So… so…"

"So what did I do?" said Barney.

"Yeah, that's it. What the hell did you *do*, man?"

"I tried to help a man I thought was my friend."

"Some friend." The incredulous expression on Mojica's face almost made Barney laugh, but he could not actually laugh, not in this place.

"Yeah, that about sums it up," said Barney. He reasoned that Mojica was not here to help him. Draw him out, maybe; play good cop and get him to say something that would rationalize a quick kill.

"Nobody who's a friend would leave you in this kinda mess. It's bad, it's like…" Mojica's hand sought a small metal crucifix around his neck. "You know?"

"Like, spiritually bad."

"Yeah. And bad for business. Not *profesional*. Not the way El Chingon does it. You see?"

Barney nodded.

"What do you think is gonna happen to you?"

"Honestly, *de veras*, I think I've been abandoned and I get to stay in this charming place until I die."

Mojica frowned as he puzzled the word "abandoned."

"*Abandonado*," said Barney.

"Ah, *sí*. You are…you are…" Mojica fought for the phrase. "You are *el hombre de las armas*—you know what that means?"

"Gunman."

"*Sí, exactamente*. You know the weapons. You hit Jesús twice in the dark while he was running. Like, expert. El Chingon could use him an expert like you."

"You bring me a job application?"

"*Es imposible*. No chance, Vance. Not while Sucio is around."

"Then, what?"

Mojica spot-checked the door several times, wrestling whether to divulge more. "Then-what, I don't know. But maybe…maybe I can find a way to get you out of here."

"Why?"

"Like I said."

"What's in it for you?"

Mojica shrugged. "I don't know that yet, neither. I think of something, I let you know."

"What about Jesús?"

Mojica performed the internationally understood *comme ci, comme ca* gesture. "Comes with the job, eh? *Dame*." He indicated that Barney should return the empty can.

Barney handed it back with live-grenade gentleness.

"Thanks," said Barney.

"De nada."

Exit Mojica.

If this was a game, it was more sophisticated than the schoolyard crap that had so far constituted Barney's incarceration. It could be one of those despair-of-hope things; something to make his torment cut more deeply, bleed more fulsomely, when the time came for killing.

The drink sure had been heaven on earth, though.

Flush-rinse-repeat.

On the days no one visited to hit him until he blacked out, Barney did not exist. Therefore, he was no one those days. Alternate days were defined by the ebb and flow of assorted pains, the occasional meal (Barney had learned to distrust feeding times as a significator of a day's passage), or a thin mock of sleep quickly ruined by the pounding heat and inadequate ventilation.

Some of those prisoners who had television sets also had air conditioning, apparently. The A-list kidnap victims. The ones with some value.

Barney had become worse off than the Old Assassin —he had ceased to exist even though he had a mission: escape before his captors tired of him and flushed him permanently, no rinse, no repeat. He had to withdraw, cocoon and marshal his remaining energies before he wasted away to his own shadow.

He would not be missed in a world full of non-people, of unlife, of zombie rote and casual strife.

Flush-rinse-repeat.

She was abducted, Carl had told him. Lie Number One.

There's nobody else I can trust in a shitstorm like this, Carl had told him. Sucker play.

Carl had done an excellent job of appearing weak and lacking in practical resources; another brilliant performance. Barney should have tipped when he noticed Carl was more conversant in Spanish than he ought to have been, particularly when he was yelling at Jesús.

Carl was deliberately vague about this so-called "Felix Rainer" guy—probably a pseudo—because he knew Barney would automatically accept the clandestine. Carl had *counted* on Barney underestimating him. Further, he had depended upon Barney overestimating his own cleanup capabilities in the daddy role.

Carl had played the Erica ace, showing a photo and relying upon Barney's perception of her to further make Carl appear to be the vulnerable gringo, at which point Barney had thought nobody would ever fox him like that.

Carl had been far too casual with the amputated finger that was presented as Erica's. He had whipped it out for dramatic effect like a bauble from a vending machine, choking up and artfully misdirecting Barney's scrutiny.

Carl had provided an armored limousine, acting like it was no biggie. The wildness of Mexico had neatly masked that magic trick.

Carl and Estrella were a conduit of intel back to El Chingon and his crew. They weren't having sex in their cheap hotel; they were comparing notes on Barney, and Estrella had reported their conclusions via cellphone like a good little spy. Some random factor or unscheduled mishap had altered Estrella's profile so that she could be sacrificed. It was what she was for. So the woman actually named Salvación had been lied to as well. Big surprise, there.

Carl should have been a lot more shocked to find his bar-bunny gutted and bled out. Instead, he let Barney direct the immediate action.

When they went to make the money drop, Carl had asked *do you really need to have that gun?* Uh-huh.

Despite his training in Basic, despite target practice in Iraq, Carl had handled Barney's .45 like an amateur to reinforce Barney's view of him as someone who needed saving.

And Barney, fool to the end, had *asked* to see the picture of Erica.

You remember how I used to be, Carl had told him. *I was a world-class fuckup. Still am.* But he was good enough at play-acting to win Barney a stay-over in the hole, so who was the real fuckup, here?

At least…wing 'em or something. By god, Carl had actually instructed Barney to shoot—and Barney had.

Carl's check was growing bigger, line by line.

The speech about how marrying Erica was the only good thing Carl had ever done—all made up.

The instructions on the phone—not coaching. Erica talking. Her script all along.

Flush-rinse-repeat.

Barney's status as a non-person was confirmed when the man Mojica had called El Chingon, the boss, showed up in person to describe the ways in which Barney had become a null quantity in the universe.

He entered Barney's room with Sucio poised behind him at respectful, subordinate distance like a giant sumo attack dog.

"That big sonofabitch comes near me again," said Barney, "and you bet I'll bite his goddamned nose off this time."

"Sucio is understandably upset at the pointless death

of his brother—not his cousin, as erroneously reported. Family means a lot to him. To us all."

"Spare me the platitudes. You're sitting on hostages for money and calling it business. At least Sucio is honestly criminal."

Sucio smiled with misplaced pride. It was not a pleasant sight. He lacked the equipment to appreciate oxymorons.

"Indeed, that is the crux of your situation, sir. Whatever your real name is. You have no *familia*. No connections of any kind. No traceable history. I have checked; wasted my time. I was misled by your good friend Carl to believe you might have some value to your government as a covert agent, some sort of subterranean asset better kept secret. It turns out you have no such worth. No one I have contacted has ever heard of you, even under the list of alleged aliases I had compiled. It is a situation I don't find myself in very often: You have no value to us."

It was impossible and pointless to explain to this man with the lazy eye that Barney's assumed reputation was more a matter of attitude, of a persona he preferred to project in order to insulate himself from the mundane. It was an air others imposed upon him, and rather than actively cultivate it, he merely did little to countermand it. His current status was backhanded proof that he wasn't such a badass after all, right?

"Great," he said, sullenly. There was no hope to be found here. "Then let's just wrap this up; I'll grab my bindle and hit the road." Again, Barney suffered the problem of which of El Chingon's eyes to track when actually looking at him.

"Not possible. Unlike most of our clients and guests, it is not wise to release you, and doing so would gain us nothing. Keeping you gains us nothing, except in the modest sense of payback where Sucio's late brother is concerned."

"Then end this," Barney said. "You know you're going to, anyway."

El Chingon shook his head. He was already perspiring from the humid closeness of the room. "That's just it. For someone to be as resilient to the tactics of interrogation as you indicates that perhaps we do not know the entire story yet. Maybe there are other options."

"I thought you were a smart businessman," said Barney. "You aren't offering me anything one way or the other, except maybe a quick death versus more of *this* bullshit."

"And you appear to have nothing to offer either. That's tragic. Under different circumstances I might have been able to make use of your abilities. But you no doubt see my dilemma, there. I have to be able to trust my functionaries or the system breaks down."

"Oh, I completely sympathize," said Barney, rolling his eyes, signaling *you can go any time, now.*

The Boss made an invisible decision and departed the room with no social amenities. He was an executive in stalemate, a condition to which executives are particularly allergic. He'd be stuck there…unless things changed, or got worse.

Flush-rinse-repeat.

Things got worse.

The next time Sucio showed up in Barney's quarters, he was alone, he was drunk, and he had brought along a pair of duck-billed tin snips.

All of Barney's fingers and toes went on high alert. His penis tried to retreat up into his chest cavity.

The tin snips were rusty, and had dried blood on them.

Sucio's alcohol-glazed eyes were dilated with some more potent form of chemical pick-me-up.

Once the door was closed and locked, Sucio began muttering *chinga tu puta madre hijo de puta mierda capullo gilipollas imbecil cacho cabron*…and so on, unending. He was steam-pressurizing toward critical mass.

Barney backed into his corner. If he could stand on his head, he might have a chance of looping the chain around the thick folds of Sucio's pack-of-franks neck. Or he could vapor-lock like a trapped cat awaiting an inevitable and unavoidable beating. Maybe he could run his own forehead into the wall fast enough to kill himself before Sucio got to take his pleasure. But Sucio was a skilled torturer, knew the moves, and most crucially, knew how to play the anticipation of extreme pain and life-thieving damage.

Sucio paused in his dress-down of Barney's lineage, sexuality and potty habits to sample an amyl nitrate popper, which snapped his focus clear with cardiac paddle speed.

Jesús was mentioned several times by name, alongside the word *venganza*. Alongside other words indicating rage, vendetta, payback time.

Then he did something exceptionally surreal: He checked his watch, a Cartier tank chronograph inlaid with mother-of-pearl that no doubt came as a free prize from a previous victim.

"*Diez minutos, joto*," he said.

Barney did not care whether he meant ten minutes to live, or that ten minutes of torture were coming. All of Barney's attention was focused on making his own adrenals squirt.

.When Sucio came in like a bullet train Barney was able to stop him short by saying, "Hey, Sucio—that's a *woman's* watch, man."

Confusion clouded Sucio's anger, then redoubled it.

Sucio roared in for the kill, and Barney nailed him in the left eye with the long-forgotten copy of *¡Alarma!*

A lot of things had to fall into place for that one desperate bet to work. But he had to chance it.

Drunk, overconfident from the past beatings he had administered, Sucio would be easy to provoke, and probably never more vulnerable than he was now, alone, almost completely out of control.

El Chingon had explained to Barney his lack of barter value. If Barney did not strike right-goddamn-now, even restrained and at such a major disadvantage, he might not get another opportunity.

The *¡Alarma!* was about thirty pages of blackly thumbed newsprint—limp pages, no staples. The word "tabloid" originated in the pharmaceutical industry to denote proper dosages in smaller tablets; it was quickly hijacked by newspapers to mean more info, smaller package, and came to refer to the size of the paper itself, or half-broadsheet size. *¡Alarma!* was the next step down—"compact" size, or about an inch smaller than tabloid.

Barney'd taken this furred and gray copy of a paper about the heft of a thin Sunday supplement and rolled it up into a tube, as tightly as he could compress it, in the hope that this object might make a good weapon. It was all he had.

He jammed it into Sucio's eye now and twisted, the paper edges cutting Sucio's eyelid. The big man howled. Before he could fall back, Barney rapped him sharply across the bridge of the nose, breaking it, bringing a glurt of nasal blood.

Barney's plan was to bring his improvised stick up, hard, under Sucio's jaw for a possible kill, or use it as a ram to drive Sucio's Adam's apple through the back of his neck. But Sucio's skin was like rhinoceros hide or leather toughened by salt. This guy was used to having his nose broken, and the sight of his own blood was no deterrent, as it would have been with a normal human, thus losing Barney that critical split second.

Sucio hoisted Barney into a brutal chokehold and held him aloft. The tendons in Barney's neck snapped audibly, like misfired popcorn. No use in whacking Sucio's bald, corrugated head; that would be like trying to knock down the wall.

Plus, Barney was notably weakened, his response zone eroded, his countermove time all used up.

After nearly a minute of asphyxiation and a possible crushed esophagus, most of the starch drained out of Barney's brilliant plan, and he belonged to Sucio, who worked him over the way a chef pounds a cut of beef.

Barney regained enough sense to realize his own gun, his stolen .45, was jammed up against his front teeth, which recorded the vibration of the hammer cocking.

"You like this gun, eh?" Sucio growled. "You kiss it goodbye, because you ain't never gonna shoot it again, *pinche gringo*."

That seemed a bizarre threat for Sucio to make; perhaps he had intended something a bit more acidic?

Barney did not have the chance to inquire. Sucio pistol-whipped him with his own gun for nearly a quarter of an hour, mangling Barney's face to raw burger.

Barney never felt Sucio amputate his right index finger with the tin snips. His trigger finger.

By the time Sucio repeated the procedure on Barney's left index finger, Barney had passed beyond feeling simple pain. He did hear the liquid cellophane sound of the blades meeting through his flesh, though, and the more arid sound of them dividing bone like brittle chalk.

Some time after that, Mojica entered Barney's room long enough to cauterize the damage of amputation using a propane torch. Barney's fingers were nowhere to be found. Mojica considered his own fingers—he still had a full set—and scuttled out as fast as possible, making sure he was not observed.

At least, that was what Barney thought he saw. Funny, he could smell burning flesh, but he couldn't feel his hands at all.

The next thing Barney saw were the maggots, busily feeding on his hands, where his index fingers used to live. That was all right. The little buggers would eat the necrotic tissue. They were nasty, but they were protein. He might eat them himself, if he ever woke up again.

Surely this was less traumatic than being shot in the head.

Maybe that came next.

❖

Of all his freedom scenarios, Barney had not antici-pated leaving the place he had come to call the Bleeding Room on his face, being dragged by one foot.

A foot that was no longer encased in the unforgiving leg shackle.

Assorted parasites had been at work on the rawed flesh of his leg. Where the cuff had secured him now felt like a third degree burn.

He was experiencing pain, and was therefore alive, perhaps delirious. One of his eyes was swollen shut and crusted. His skeleton felt disconnected. Wounds everywhere. Teeth rocking in their gum beds. Brain hammering. Heart still pumping, blood still moving, even if a lot of it was vacating the premises. Dizziness, disorientation. He felt he had puked and shat so much that if you looked down his throat, you'd see light.

They—someone—dragged his dead ass out, down steps. Sacked his head. Stinky bag, probably the same one from his earlier trip. He was in the van again, the one in which he and Carl had been taken. Carl's past few pay periods, by comparison, had probably been less debilitating. This time, he was not around to grab Barney's hand and drag him up out of the smoth-ering sand.

The unseen road trip that followed was not measur-able in units of time. The only clock Barney possessed was his own heartbeat. It could have been a week. He had to remain inside of himself, sequestered. He thought of his organs, stubbornly churning away in spite of the memo that came down saying *just die*. Maybe they were taking him to a *clínica*. Maybe they were driving him home. Maybe Sucio had slipped up, gone overboard, and now they had to doctor him.

Yeah, right.

More bumpy roads and more roughhouse dragging. When the bag was yanked off his head Barney was staring bleary-eyed at the Rio Satanas, from the top of the bridge. Sucio was sporting a bandage beneath a patch on one eye. The glowering orb of the setting sun made everything shade crimson and blurred Barney's own light-sensitive vision, but he recognized Mojica, standing back a pace, politic. He did not feel the usual waves of animal hatred broiling off Sucio; the big man seemed to have clamped down and toughened up, all business, curses shelved, silent again.

Sucio grabbed Barney by the scruff and the crotch and heaved him over the edge. No parting insult, no quip. Barney hit the oil-sheened surface of the mulchy water inelegantly and headfirst, sinking to brush the tar-like aggregate bottom, sucking a lungful of turbid liquid with floating chunks in it, then slowly ascending from his own buoyancy toward filtered light. He had a flash thought of his goldfish, under Armand's stewardship, back in another world called Los Angeles. If you didn't clean the aquarium for a couple of months and allowed the mold and algae to build up, shut off the filtration system so the fish were swimming in ammoniac piss and liquefied gray shit, then dunked your entire head into the tank, it would probably be a lot like this.

Back on the bridge a brief discourse ensued in Spanish between Mojica and Sucio concerning the number of minutes left to Barney's life. Barney caught bits of it as he bobbed, water draining from one ear while it filled the other. One said Barney was dead, the other said Barney wasn't, and it went back and forth, in the manner of gang taunts, no matter either way, a kind of *yes-he-is, no-he's-not* time-passer.

Barney could imagine the sizzling fire-coal deep in Sucio's good eye. He'd had hurt the huge enforcer, hurt him visibly and humiliatingly, and *nobody* hurt Sucio, that was clearly a rule in their world.

Barney floated on the surface, face-down, no bubbles.

"*Mira*," said Mojica. "*Muerte, carnal.*"

Sucio unlimbered his revolver, aimed down at the floating body, and spent all six rounds.

Barney rotated in the water, surrounded by a corona of freshly freed blood.

"*Now* he is," said Sucio, turning back to the van.

A disembodied woman's voice seemed to ask Barney, *Where are my children?*

He had holes in him; that much he knew. He was hit. He had been hit a few times before, in his previous life.

Shock trauma took over once he ran dry of endorphins; he could not feel a thing. Bullet impact had flipped him over in the water, and instead of drowning, he was more or less afloat and still drawing air along with the occasional mouthful of sewage. He rejected the bilge. Autonomic functions had taken over and he did not think about willfully breathing. He worried in the abstract about taking on water—holes in a rowboat could sink it—but for the most part he was far away from his physical body, occasionally observing it from the distant place to which his mind had been exiled. But all he could see was the sky at dusk. The world seemed aflame.

The Rio Satanas was devilish in its commitment to seek the sea, or other, fresher tributaries. Sunrise, sunset and the tidal pull of the moon exerted their influence to provide a kind of current. He revolved, in the manner of a lazy sunbather in a hotel pool. He saw the ransom bridge receding, only once, before it became too dark to gauge distance.

This is how life ends.

Life ends not in triumph and fulfillment, but depletion and ignominy. Barney was used up, tapped out, leaking sentience from holes in his body, run dry of humanity, reduced to a kind of absurd chattel for the amusement of psychopaths. Alive or dead, he no longer existed; perhaps never existed before, except as a shade of himself, a suggestion of a person, a conglomeration of tics and traits and moot statistics, none quite diverting. It is easy to blow large holes in a tissue-thin simulacrum of life.

His murderers had not only denied his humanity, but contravened his existence. He was not important enough to keep, nor unimportant enough to cut free. He was nothing, and the universe at large did not care about teaching him spurious moral lessons. Given a fresh, whole body and a set of guns, he could destroy everyone who ever did him wrong, but what would that change? Nothing. Because he was nothing; he mattered not, on the big scale.

There was no balance to restore. Nobody would care. He was not a religious man; *pie in the sky by and by when you die.* He had structured his life so that he was never owed anything by anyone, so by what right would he claim recompense?

Again his fractured perception registered the dis-

tant sound of a woman in tears. A local: *"¡O hijos mios!"*
Perhaps Barney was a lost child, floating home.

I have no one, the Old Assassin had told him. *I care
for no one. And I'm cared for by no one. So all I have is
what I can do.*

Barney could not *do* anything except bob along in
the disgusting mulch of the river. Perceptions ebbing.
The quick hallucination, dream, or flashback. Not like
the legend—no clip reel of your life's deeds and mis-
deeds unspooling before your semi-conscious mind;
no tunnel of light; zero choir. The dull pulse of biologically blocked pain, radiating like a distant, dying sun.

This is how life ends.

Life ends when you are totally free.

Something was chewing on his foot. Maybe a sump rat
the size of a terrier; maybe one of those monster cat-
fish from the Amazon, a nine-foot-long killer mutated
by the toxic waste in the river.

It nibbled on Barney's bare heel and he feebly kicked
it away, splashing black water.

Deep inside his mind, Barney was startled—a sign
of life? What?! Something as simple as *don't eat me,
you monster?*

Another nibble and he lashed out again, completely
without thinking. His lungs were still stubbornly
drawing air in clotted rasps.

A bolt of pain scissored up his leg and somehow
located nerve receptors long since shut down.

*Oww, fucker, I need that toe for a tag; leave me
alone.*

Barney recalled the kids he had seen huffing paint,
glazed and otherdimensional, casually homicidal. His

strange hallucinations and prolapsed volition could be attributed to the poisonous bouillabaisse of the river-that-was-not-a-river, his new home. The toxic waste had recombined into luxurious new forms, folding its plasmas, infiltrating his metabolism through every bullet hole, gash and wound. It backed up in his liver and kidneys to percolate and birth new concentrated cocktails of bio-active excreta. All human activity generated some form of waste; Barney came to see himself, during his few lucid episodes, as just one more form of hazardous leftover, dumped in with all the others.

His new world was very cosmopolitan. There was a little bit of everything in it: corrosives, explosives, solvents, mercury, lead, petroleum, ashes, antifreeze, propane, caustics, pesticide, acetone, benzene, ammonia, lye, alkalies and alkalines, formaldehyde, xylene …the whole encyclopedia of wanton chemical hazard, all of it blenderized with megatons of unprocessed human sewage.

This was Mexico's version of the Love Canal.

Along the way, Barney had contributed his own throw-off: perspiration, blood, Numbers One and Two, mucus, saliva, skin flakes, but not a single tear, or so he believed.

The sky floating above him assumed alien hues.

He still could not feel his hands.

He dreamt of a party.

No, fiesta, down here it would be a fiesta.

Piñatas, refrescos. Helado—ice cream.

Gaily attired people. Music.

Someone's wedding, or birthday, or anniversary. *Boda, cumpleaños, aniversario.*

Unless it was *his* party.

A loose-limbed puppet carved of dark wood, with a baked-apple face, spoke to him in a language he did not understand.

The puppet was wearing a battered straw hat; a neckerchief.

Its voice sounded a billion years old.

Barney began to levitate toward the sun, which spiked in through his slitted eyes like firebrands.

The sun was all he could see, as Icarus saw it when his wax wings melted.

Muy caliente. Very hot.

If he closed his eyes, they would weld shut and he would never see anything again. His pupils dilated to microdots, overwhelmed.

The puppet droned away, unseen now. Whatever it was talking about sounded very bad.

Stupid puppet.

Barney was inside the Bleeding Room again.

Not the same as before; this was a madhouse where he was restrained, sliced up, tortured with needles. Bound down, hurling up his own guts. Beaten and stretched and bound again. Force-fed vile fluids and tormented by an army of imps who poked and prodded, cut away his flesh and seeded it with salt.

In his mind, he retreated even deeper, hauling ass down a cobwebbed corridor—man, he had *never* been in *this* room!—and slamming a door, then finding another artery, moving swiftly, slamming another door until he was lost in the catacomb-pit of his own brain.

Outside, they continued to raze his flesh. Whatever they wanted, Barney did not have it.

Down deep in the catacombs, Barney confronted one of his worst personal fears—that he was really in an asylum, irretrievably insane, violent and bound down in max-lock, trapped and screaming inside his own ruptured head, unable to get a message to the outside world.

Lunacy, coma.

The second Bleeding Room made the first seem like a high-roller suite in Vegas, the kind you get comped when the hotel wants to clean out your bank.

Not food, but *cuisine*; hookers on-call, all the amenities. No Sucio. No betrayers at all, in fact.

In the second Bleeding Room all the inquisitioners were completely faceless. There was no crime, no clue as to your sin, and zero appeal. It was pretty much an atheist's perfect picture of Hell.

Barney fled, slammed another door, locked it, went deeper.

Found another door, leading downward.

It was very dark at the end of the corridor.

The dead thing was clad in a moldering priest's outfit, and had patches of moss on its head instead of hair. Its head was a skull glistening with gelid rot. It hectored Barney in a voice that had the sound of withered dry reeds, clicking. It extended skeletal fingers over his supine form and tried to touch him. Unable to move, Barney tried to will away physical contact. A squirming grub fell out of the creature's eye socket and landed on Barney's chest, where it vanished in a corkscrew twist down one of the bullet holes there. The holy-collared gravewalker tried to smear stale blood on Barney's head and its reach broke the *mantilla* of cobwebs in which it was shrouded.

Get away from me. Take your superstitions and get away. Sell your lies somewhere else.

Like a pestersome insect, the damned thing continued to hover and natter, its off-center jawbone waggling nonsense and dislodging tomb dust, which sifted down through baleful light to coat Barney's open eyes. Apparently this annoying specter was going to yammer on until its script was done, and Barney briefly wondered if he could grab the tarnished bone crucifix that depended from its jackstraw neck and turn it to use as a stabbing weapon; anything to stem the tide of gibberish.

Oh, for a firearm to blast this apparition into crypt dirt.

The third Bleeding Room came as a total surprise.

Barney saw low beamed ceilings and roof of thatch. The predominant odors were cooking food, incense, and something akin to ground stone. An unseen clock ticked ponderously.

He tried to sit up on the narrow bed and was slammed down by nausea and his body's inability to do what he told it. His muscles did not obey.

The clock became maddening—an actual, undeniable measure of time, unless he was merely making all this up in his shell-shocked mind.

"I see you dream," said a voice. "*Las pesdillas*. The movement of the eyes."

"REM," Barney said. His voice had been taken. All that was left was a dry tumbleweed whisper.

His consciousness was a treacherous ascent over booby-trapped ice with a thousand hidden traps. One foothold wrong, and he would tumble. Funny that he saw an ice field; he had expected sand dunes to the horizon.

"*Ariem?*" echoed the brittle voice. "That is not your name; how you are called—*¿como se llama?*"

The horrible puppet from the nightmare fiesta hovered over him, and Barney blacked out.

When he awoke again, he was still in the third Bleeding Room, with the infernal clock ticking away.

The puppet moved toward him with a disjointed gait, as though inexpertly manipulated, its feet several inches from the ground.

"Ah, *amigo*," it said.

It was not a marionette, but a man. A small, wizened man whose face was a map of desert sun-wrinkles, who smiled with gapped teeth that nonetheless lit up his mahogany countenance. An older man in the back third of a life that looked as if it had been equally rich in regret and joy.

"You are back with us," the man said. "The saints, if there are such things, love you."

Yeah, *that* idea was a laff riot.

Barney struggled to say *who*, to ask *where*.

"Shh, *tranquilo*," said the man. "I am Jorge Estrada Gutierrez Maria Conejo Juan Sanchez Valasquez de los Piedras. I am called Mano." He held up his hand, of which he possessed only one. "*Solamente un mano*," he said by way of illumination.

" 'Of the stones?' " said Barney.

"*Si, 'de los piedras,' *" he said. "My calling. I find the rocks. Agates, much opal......what do you call them, geodes? All kinds of rocks."

"Rockhound."

"I think I have heard that word..." His brows knit, pondering the meaning.

"Miner?"

"No." Mano worked his tongue over his teeth, searching for a descriptive in the way one might speak to a child. "Pretty rocks."

"Gems, jewelry?" Forming words seemed a new challenge to Barney. They tasted rather good.

"Yes, *al veces*. I dug up the diamond my son gave his *esposa* for their wedding. Some silver, some onyx, some…how is it called? Apache tear. *El ojo de tigre*. Yes. Here. *Bebes*. You must drink."

He offered a tin cup containing tea, strong, bitter, laced with herbs. Later he would alternate this with fruit juice and plenty of water. Swallowing, for Barney, had become a newly learned behavior. Mano patiently guided him through it.

"My second son's second wedding anniversary," said Mano. "That is where we found you, on the bank of the Arroyo de la Llorona, where there used to be very good fishing. The fish, they have since died or gone elsewhere; the water is *veneno, tosigo…*"

"Poison."

"The Arroyo feeds from many sources before it changes—" Mano dovetailed his hands, or hand and stump "—to the Rio Bramante, and seeks the sea. You were put in the Arroyo somewhere to the north, and— *buena suerte*—found your way to us."

"*El accidente*," said Barney.

"But for your wounds I would believe you," Mano said sternly, like a parent. "Four bullets in you. Two remain. *Los dedos…*" Mano held up his only index finger and wiggled it.

It was pointless to lie. "A very bad man took them."

Mano nodded. "Took them, then gave them back to you. I would not wish to meet such a man."

"What do you mean, he gave them back?"

Mano seemed to be having trouble, chewing on how to properly express what he knew. "In your body," he finally said. "You passed them *en clínica.*"

Sucio had forced Barney to swallow his own severed fingers.

Barney lost his grip on reality, and sailed down to embrace the blackness once more.

Broth, now, stronger. Barney felt it flow into him.

"When was I in the hospital? The *clínica?*"

Night, now, cooler, with cicadas razzing outside.

"Doctor Mendez says you are dead, then you are alive, then dead, and alive again. He wishes for city doctors, big *equipamiento*, but he is a very good and kind man. He fix your cuts, help your hands."

Barney's mutilations were anonymous in a fat swaddle of bandages.

"How long?"

Mano calculated. "*Dos semanas, minimo.*" Two weeks at least. "My son's wife, she prays for you every night."

No doubt to choke off the morbid idea that Barney's appearance, floating right into the middle of her anniversary celebration, might be a bad omen. *Los Catolicos* were superstitious that way.

"It was her, Soleil, who insisted the priest give you last rites. I said no, you are not yet a dead man. But she insisted."

So much for the grim specter in the clerical collar.

Mano held several vials of pills. "These, says the doctor, are for infection. These, for fever. These, for …something else. They say when to take them. You must take some now, yes?"

"Yes. More water, please—*mas agua, por favor*."

"You speak the Spanish."

Barney would have held thumb and forefinger an inch apart; would have said *un poquito, muy mal*, but he no longer had forefingers. Sucio had jammed them down his gullet and probably suffocated him until he gulped. What was left eventually emerged from his colon. Mano had seen them, perhaps salvaged them. Barney did not want to see them (at least not right this moment) and did not know if he even had the heart left to ask after their fate, just in case some nurse had flushed them down a toilet.

One of the pills was obviously for pain, which Barney determined by squinting at the labels. His guts felt bulldozed and his body felt hotly gravid with infection. He knew he was in the midst of biologically processing an unknown smorgasbord of organic contaminants. His neck and throat burned, his injuries restricted his movements, and it felt like a toothache had nested in his right eye.

"Why are you doing all this?" he asked Mano.

Mano just smiled as Barney drifted away.

Projectile vomiting in the middle of the next night. The soles of his feet felt aflame or peeled by acid. Blurred vision. Phantom pain from his hands. The bullet wounds radiating heat, swollen, growing ripe.

Mano held the puke bucket, wrapped Barney's feet in aloe, administered eyedrops from Dr. Mendez, rebandaged his ruined hands, drained and dressed the gunshot wounds.

It took Barney more than a week to work his stamina up to handling solid food.

I was dead once, Mojica had said. *They killed my ass. And I'm still here.*

The unseen clock kept ticking. Barney was always aware of it, but the passage of linear time remained a befuddlement, clouded by shifting tempo and sudden reversals. He imagined (or dreamt he could see through his closed eyelids) the second Bleeding Room, obviously a minimalist ward in some rural medical facility. No beeping machines, very basic—IV stands, worn but clean linens, and a broad toadlike man (Dr. Mendez?) leaning close, his wide, thick-lipped face speaking with no audio. He looked stern but kind. He gingerly lifted one of Barney's mangled hands. Barney saw in great detail what would later be described as a *crude transverse cut of the proximal phalange above the metacarpophalangeal joint, or halfway between the base knuckle and first finger knuckle.*

His trigger finger, gone. He had swallowed it.

Barney could not feel a thing as Dr. Mendez disinfected a small row of sutures on the finger stump, where dying flesh had been trimmed and closed over the protruding stub of bone.

Sucio could have taken his thumbs, or both his hands, to incapacitate Barney more hideously. There was a sinister motive in his choice, a perverse editorialization. He could have applied his cutters to the penis or testicles, the eyelids, the tongue. Instead, he had unmanned Barney in a way that would do the most damage on the inside; obliterating Barney's carefully guarded sense of self, the identity that even Mojica had perceived—Barney was *el hombre de las armas* no more.

Mano was the proprietor of a modest gem and min-

eral shop in the district of Xochimilco, once on the
outskirts of Mexico City but now incorporated into its
urban sprawl. Many of his repeat customers were
Mexican wrestlers of considerable fame and standing
in the Lucha Libre community, patrons of an adjacent
shop where a retired grappler named Tigre Loco designed and manufactured masks, costumes and a few
props for the wildly popular bouts held at Arena
Coliseo and other venues. The luchadors spread the
word, and their more well-heeled friends sought out
Mano for handcrafted jewelry, hammered silver and
uniquely designed mounts for his meticulously cut and
polished stones.

For most of the years of his life, Mano had grimly
watched the fashion of kidnapping wax and corrupt
Mexico like a metastasizing cancer. He had been
robbed at gunpoint seventeen separate times (successfully and unsuccessfully), mugged on the street, and
randomly assaulted by the cocky, the desperate and
the drug-addicted. But these miscreants were few
when balanced against the average Mexican citizen, so
Mano remained in business, conceding to grated windows, iron doors, alarms.

One abortive robbery attempt was rendered almost
hilarious when three punks entered Mano's empo-
rium with one malfunctioning Saturday Night Special
among them, and proceeded to yell threats because
they'd seen too many movies. Next door in Tigre's
were no fewer than seven wrestlers who heard the
commotion, bracketed Mano's store from front and
rear, and proceeded to pummel the fluid out of the
trio of would-be highwaymen. This was neither fake
brawl nor stunt show, and the kids were all hospital-

ized with a wealth of broken noses, lost teeth, splintered bones, concussions and dislocations. Typically, the wrestlers were hailed as local superheroes and no lawsuits materialized. This was not the United States.

Mano settled into his role as Barney's caretaker, relating such stories as these in a calm monotone as though telling tales around a campfire. The kind of stories a friend tells a friend as a matter of course. His daughter-in-law continued her prayers and vigils for Barney's recovery.

When Barney mentioned the ghostly woman's voice he had heard while in the river, Mano told him three different versions of the La Llorona myth, after which the tributary had been named.

It was a fundamental parable in Mexican culture, percolating through many iterations throughout all of Latin America and the southwestern United States. The Weeping Woman, the Crying Woman, or the Woman in White was the ghost of a mother forced to murder her children, nearly always by drowning them in a waterway. The stories varied as to her motivation, but her curse was to haunt riverbanks, calling out in a mournful voice in an attempt to re-locate her lost little ones.

In one version of the story, Mano said that La Llorona was a woman named María, the "secret wife" of a man who jilts her for his higher-profile legitimate spouse. Enraged, she drowns their children and later kills herself in grief. In Heaven, God asks her where her children are. She does not know. In typical punitive pique, God condemns her to walk the earth in search of them, making the legend a cautionary boogeyman fable, since La Llorona might drown your wandering kids to replenish her family.

In a more tragic vein, La Llorona is said to have drowned her children to spare them from starving to death, or to preempt their death in an oncoming flood sure to kill them. In sorrow, she searches eternally to get them back.

More lurid versions of the legend have La Llorona stabbing her children to death and confronting their father in a blood-soaked nightgown; drowning bastards she bore as a prostitute, or killing her husband, then committing suicide out of remorse. Her manifestations—for anyone unfortunate enough to actually see her, sufficient grounds to mark the witness for death—included her in a flowing all-white or all-black gown, sometimes skeletal or with swirling black pits for eyes. One version has an ever-tetchy God sending her back to Earth with the head of a horse. Her signature wailing cry is sometimes said to be heard only by those about to die themselves.

"I heard her speak," Barney said. "She said, '*Drink from my breast, for I am your mother.*'"

"Impossible," said Mano, his weathered visage dispensing an avuncular tolerance. "It is a myth, a legend. Not a real thing. You rest, now."

"Mano," Barney said some days later. "Do you have a gun?"

But Mano was not in the room. Barney realized he had been rehearsing aloud, trying to keep the question in his mind so he could sound less like a lunatic when the little man reappeared. He said it over and over, so he would not lose track.

The extent of Barney's exercise in the better part of a month was limited to a half-situp in bed, which generally cramped his stomach something awful, and trips to the bathroom, reliant on Mano for mobility. Today Barney was alone in the house while Mano tended his business, or had possibly gone on an expedition to dig up new stones for cutting and polishing. Until recently, one of his sons or their wives drew babysitting duty, but none of them spoke a lick of English, and when Barney tried to communicate in his pidgin Spanish, it was usually hopeless, reducing them all to grunts, gestures and grade-school monosyllables.

He got the feeling that Mano's family (none of whom lived with him, and that in itself was unusual for Mexico) did not approve of this half-dead gringo guest. They were all kind, but saw to Barney's needs with a palpable air of burden. Barney guessed that the La Llorona anecdote had leaked. Being Catholic, they would race to distance themselves from the marked man; *get thee behind me, Barney!* Being Mano's children, they would diddle rosaries and perhaps even go as far as to light a votive in church for the stranger, but as far as they were concerned, he was an agent of darkness sideswiping the *familia*. Barney noticed for the first time the absence of dogma-specific rickrack in Mano's home. It could be that the vague rift he sensed between Mano and the rest of his brood had to do with his indifference to their faith. The few things Mano had mentioned about his late wife indicated that her death coincided with the point at which he and God had parted company.

Mano was a much rarer commodity, a religious man unencumbered by religious beliefs. What he cherished was abundantly on display: his stones, rescued from riverbeds and caliche, lovingly turned and polished, doing quiet honor to the very planet from which they all had sprung.

Barney's first attempt to navigate toward the door of his little sickroom was either a catastrophe or a comedy skit.

It took him nearly ten minutes to upright himself in the bed. Every muscle in his arms felt sprung and dysfunctional, corroded by toxins into rusty obsolescence. His inner ear's balance system fouled him up when he tried to stand. He managed two clomping, Frankensteinian steps and then took a header as the room swam out of focus around him. He destroyed a spool table he tried to clutch on the way down to the floor, and lay boneless in the debris like an infant awaiting a diaper change. With a drunken sense of mission he used his teeth to shred the bandages from one hand and stared blankly at his truncated forefinger. The stump was lumpy and awkward; not a human tool any more. It would offend anyone who saw it.

Worse, the big, bloody Q-Tips at the ends of his arms made it futile when it came to cleaning or feeding himself. He was entirely dependent on Mano's good graces, and he hated himself for feeling beholden.

Worse still, when Mano returned, the old man acted like it was all no big deal, calmly righting Barney and cleaning up the mess. Mano actually *liked* this lost soul, for absolutely no reason Barney could see. Perhaps Barney had become a project. Perhaps Mano got some unspecified satisfaction he could not reap from his many relatives. Perhaps he was a genuine samaritan, although Barney's experience admitted no such largesse, dismissing it as a weakness. Barney's life had largely coalesced around compensating for the weaknesses of others; doing the jobs others could not bring themselves to do. Being taken care of was new to him, and slightly scary. Uncharted terrain. It disrupted all Barney thought he knew about human nature.

He wondered what he could do for the old man in return, if he regained the capability to do anything, ever again.

"Mano, do you have a gun?"

"A *gonn*?" He said it like *cone*.

"A firearm. Sidearm. Pistol. *La pistola*."

Mano produced the rickety shooting iron used during the spectacularly misconceived attempt to rob his store. Barney examined it gently with one unbandaged, three-fingered hand.

It was a short-barreled, seven-shot .32 caliber Omega revolver with two bullets still asleep in the cylinder and nodes of rust on the trigger. The top left side featured a stamp of Mercury or some other Roman god. It was a fifty-buck junk gun, a real Ring of Fire special, as likely to explode in your hand as drop the hammer shy of the primer. A lot of crap similar to it had floated through the shooting range's repair and sales department even though such safety-last weapons had been illegal in California since the Gun Control Act of 1968, a misfired piece of legislation that provided a handy loophole by which the *parts* for such guns could still be shipped into the state. It was the kind of randy hot-pocket pistol a junkie would steal and try to pawn; inaccurate, cheap, easily concealed and totally dangerous. It had probably never been cleaned.

Good .32s were still classic ankle guns for law en-

forcement, who used the revolvers to backstop the
semi-autos that were now pretty standard sidearms.
Barney recalled reading that in the early 1920s, police
officers in the deep South switched to .38 caliber carry
guns from .32s because they believed cocaine made
Negroes impervious to the smaller rounds.

Barney dumped the shells—pirate loads of disrep-
utable manufacture—and carefully threaded his right
middle finger through the trigger guard, grasped, and
tried to cycle the hammer. It stuttered back about
three millimeters, then relaxed as his hand gave out
and began to bleed. It stung and throbbed like hell.
*Forty trigger pulls in thirty seconds, dry-firing…*and
Barney could not manage a single one, with his stronger
hand.

"Who you wish to shoot?" said Mano.

"Nobody," said Barney, omitting the yet. "This used
to be…*is*…my specialty. Like you with rocks."

"*Estas un malhechor?*" Mano asked this with an
utter lack of guile; his inflection made it clear that
what he was really asking was: *Are you a criminal, an
evil man, or are you misunderstood?*

Barney almost smiled. "Depends on who you ask. I
was once a soldier. I know a lot about guns. But no, not
in the way you mean."

"A great wrong has been done to you that might
cause you to become a bad man."

"A criminal, perhaps, but not a bad man. I would
not harm a man such as yourself, for instance. Yes, I
wish to do harm to those who harmed me. But it's
bigger than that. *Mas grande.* Besides, look at me,
Mano. *Mirame.* The only person I can harm is myself,
if I sit up too fast."

Blood was trickling down his wrist.

Mano tended the hand and let him hang onto the "gonn." He obviously did not want to look at it, and would probably dispose of it after today.

Another ritual that divided the calendar was the twice-weekly trip to the clinic to check in with Dr. Mendez, accomplished by Mano choreographing his assorted relatives. Nothing awaited them this time but bad news.

Dr. Mendez was dead.

The account, which unfurled in Barney's mind much like the telling of another myth, went that Dr. Mendez had left the clinic two evenings earlier, stopped his car for reasons unknown (or was carjacked), suffered a gunshot wound, was abandoned or somehow managed to drive his vehicle three miles closer to his home before crashing into a tree and bleeding to death. He was not found until the following morning.

Another physician, clearly upset at the violent end to the much-loved Dr. Mendez's life, examined Barney, drew blood, and mortared up his injuries with shaking hands. One of Sucio's bullets had nicked his right scapula; another had sundered a rib, this latter being one of the slugs still inside him. Due to its proximity to Barney's heart and the lingering hazard of bone splinters, a big-city surgery was advised. Bone hits were a fifty-fifty shot; pound for pound, most bone in the human body is as strong as steel. They could protect your internal organs, or bounce incoming bullets straight into them.

Barney kept asking the doctor, whose name was Hector Quisneros, "What kind of gun was Dr. Mendez attacked with? What kind of bullet was he shot with?"

"I don't know, but I'm sure I can find out. Why—is it relevant? It won't matter." Dr. Quisneros removed his square-rimmed steel glasses and massaged the bridge of his nose. "The police will not follow up reliably even for a citizen of Dr. Mendez's status. I'm sorry, but it's the truth."

The killer came for Barney the following night.

Dr. Quisneros had recommended a one-night maintenance stay at the clinic, perhaps longer, but Barney could already smell death on the breeze. He quickly counseled Mano to get away from his home, and keep his family clear as well. Mano stuck.

Barney lay in wait, unable to sleep, with nothing for company but the metronome ticking of the clock and the Saturday Night Special with two shots left. He feebly grasped the .32 in his unwrapped gun hand, hoping to achieve a single shot before the remaining tatters and strings of that hand fell apart. The pistol was a real piece of shit; a whore's gun. It barely mattered which side of the muzzle you were on.

Mano maddeningly deflected Barney's worry and warnings. He puttered around his home, fixed an indifferent meal, refused to entertain the crazy notion of *asesinos* in the night, and finally went to bed with no further comment.

First thought: *Mano has told somebody, and is in on it.*

Second thought: *Sucio is being thorough.*

Third, and most damning thought: What if Barney's senses had completely forsaken him? His combat smarts, his night vision, his skin alarms, his preternatural sense of the shape and threat potential of the unknown up-ahead—what if he had lost them all in the river, what if they had drained out through the many holes in his body? What if his web of plots, connections, coincidences, motives and murderers was just his fear talking out loud, or the medicine amplifying his paranoia?

To hell with all that. There was a single reality here: The bad guys knew he was alive, and sought to correct that oversight.

The stranger came just past midnight, after Mano had gone to bed. Barney felt the air shift subtly in the small house, and waited for a cautious silhouette to fill up the doorway to his little room. It was a large man—not Sucio—stinking of recently bought safari clothing and wearing a black ski mask.

The pistol he had smelled new, too. Factory lubricant still on it. The bore, almost invisible in the dim light, was a black hole waiting to suck in Barney's life first, followed by the rest of the universe.

Not a hallucination; not a fever dream.

Barney's eardrums nearly imploded from the blinding roar of discharge.

The intruder became visible in a flashbulb corona of hot yellow light, then seemed to unhinge as portions of the doorway became visible through his midsection, which disintegrated, raining blood and most of his internal organs all over Barney, who was still snapping the useless .32 with his wrecked hand, the trigger falling over and over on empty chambers and the two dud cartridges. Something in his wrist seemed to thrum, then snap like a rubber band, giving out. His own blood was already coursing down his arm.

Mano clicked on the light before the interloper's

body finished hitting the floor in a macerated sprawl, his weapon spinning into a corner. Gunsmoke clogged the room and the stink of cordite made it hard to breathe—such a huge, devastating blast in such a tiny space. Mano became visible through a haze of purple spots in Barney's vision. He stood in the doorway holding about half a mile of double-barreled shotgun that looked like an old Savage/Stevens model 311 side-by-side, with twin triggers. He had held low and given the night caller both chambers at less than four feet. The 12-gauge double-aught rounds, coming in like a hornet-swarm of eighteen .32 caliber bullets fired all at once, had blown him apart at the base of the spine. He was not going to get up.

It was a miracle Barney was not taken out, too, by the spread pattern or the velocity of pellets that have been known to punch through an adobe wall *after* bisecting a human target.

"*Esta bueno?*"

Barney was shaking. Never before had he been rattled by gunfire. Nervous, yes, from tempting fate or being boxed in; apprehensive at bad strategy, hopeless from dire situations, but never aquiver at gunfire, which he thought to be his element.

"*Amigo,*" Mano repeated, leaning the shotgun against the wall and stepping over the shredded corpse on the floor. "*Esta bueno?*"

"Yeah," Barney managed, his voice running away to a husky whisper. His eyes indicated the gun with which Mano had saved him. "Mano…what the *hell*?"

"Oh, that." Mano shrugged, smiled. "Now that, my friend, is a *gonn.*"

◦

This one was easier to figure out, now.

The killer, regardless of his muffed job status, had been a professional. An American, a stranger, a blond man with a rubescent complexion and bulletproof fake ID. Therefore, not sent by El Chingon, who probably would have sent Sucio.

Therefore, the kidnapping crew down here apparently did not yet know that Barney was still drawing breathable air.

So: the killer had been sent by Carl Ledbetter, or one of his satellites.

Why: Barney had been alive, though in dire circumstances, when Carl exited Mexico. He had probably gotten the news on Barney's disposition and decided to check hospital and clinic emergency admissions; most likely he did his entire investigation on the Internet, with the right passwords. It would be simple to take some of his share of the million bucks and invest in a guarantor, who had found the clinic in Xochimilco and sweated poor Dr. Mendez until he spilled Barney's whereabouts and died. Game, set, and match…except he had not factored in the possibility of the apparently harmless Mano packing some unsuspected heirloom firepower.

It held water as much as anything his scattered brain could conceive.

Result: Barney's security had been compromised, and everyone around him was no longer safe. Their location was now, in the parlance, "hot." *Muy caliente*.

"Mano, I have to leave this place."

Mano countered that this was not a good idea, given Barney's handicapped status.

"Mano, you and your family are in danger because of me."

Mano returned that he had been in danger before, many times, and it was not good to live in fear.

"Mano, I have to get back to the States, somehow."

Mano suggested that phoning up the American embassy in Mexico City was probably not the most efficacious course to take.

Barney's existence as a visiting foreigner was gray at best; in-country on forged documents, involved in local criminal activity, responsible, at least in theory, for several deaths. He could claim to have been mugged, attacked, or kidnapped, all documents lost, but that might surface connections to the bad guys or the wobbly architecture of his paperwork—any slip could invite unwanted scrutiny, and seal his fate. Regional law enforcement, corrupt as they were, might just dump him back into the hands of El Chingon's crew, or detain him in yet another locked room. No good.

Mano told Barney to wait, since he might have a solution. He was distressingly cryptic on what that might be.

Meanwhile, Barney had won himself a brand-new firearm.

The assassin's piece of choice turned out to be a tactical SIG P229 with a threaded barrel, probably for a silencer he never got to try—this brand of pistol, firing beefier cartridges, was known to be loud. SIGs came with decocking levers, not safeties, so they were always ready to use. With Mano's help, Barney field-stripped it and found the original .357 barrel had been swapped out to accept the Smith & Wesson .40 cartridge, a popular conversion. A Sprinco recoil reducer had been added to improve the control of rapid-fire shots—less muzzle climb, better sight recovery. That little piece of frosting could reduce the kick by half, not inconsiderable when your gun could muster over a thousand foot-pounds at impact. The single-stack hi-cap mag jutted from the butt of the gun, containing fifteen deadly bees, plus one in the pipe. Not exactly a race gun, but the owner had added a match trigger. The whole package had been refinished to be absolutely glare-proof and non-reflecting. The action was smooth as glass.

Waylaid as he was, Barney felt better just having the gun nearby.

He dozed off thinking of stimulants versus sedatives. He had to get up and moving, no matter how many leaks he sprang.

He woke up with an enormous man in a gray sharkskin business suit staring down at him. The suit barely contained him, its seams heroically restraining a cinderblock physique. His silk necktie was knotted stranglehold-tight. From the neck up his head was encased in a skin-tight lace-up mask in metallic kelly green, adorned with red vinyl flames rocketing backward. The eyeholes were teardrop-shaped and edged with more crimson, as though blood-enraged. Only the man's mouth and chin were visible; the mask was cut away and molded for that small freedom. He had a dark goatee. He stood with oaken-stout arms folded, as imposing as a Mayan statue, looking down upon Barney, godlike, with eyes the color of strong Colombian coffee.

"This," said Mano, "is El Atrocidad."

The Mexican wrestling superstar known as "The Atrocity" already held Barney in his debt. He had helped Mano dispose of the assassin's body by dumping it in the Arroyo de La Llorona. Where else?

In guttural but very serviceable English, Atrocidad
told Barney that his own wife's brother, Carlos Fuentes,
had been kidnapped in Mexico City by men who sacked
his head, stuffed him into a van, and drove him to an
unknown location where he was held in a hostage hotel
until a hefty ransom had been forked over. Carlos, too,
had suffered the loss of two fingers, and an ear, but
could still play the guitar, and, presumably, hear music.
As Atrocidad gestured, Barney saw that his massive,
knotty hands lacked fingernails.

Atrocidad had also been present at the donnybrook
inside Mano's shop. A single stiff-armed blow to the
forehead had taken the punk with the .32, breaking his
nose, freeing four of his teeth, and landing him in the
emergency ward with a skull fracture. There was the
roughhouse ballet of lucha libre—beer-bellied athletes
in elaborate, bone-crunching choreography—and then
there was actual combat; it was impossible to be adept
at one without being able to perform the other. As
Atrocidad said, the first rule is knowing how to fall
down without getting killed or landing yourself in a
wheelchair—that is, if you wanted a career as a wrestler
that lasted beyond your first bout.

Barney had actually seen El Atrocidad wrestle a few
years back at the Vatican of Mexican wrestling, Arena
Coliseo, as part of a tag team with Tiburon Negro and
Doctor Hate, a.k.a. the Black Shark and Medico Odio.
As *rudos*, bad guys, their job was to foul constantly, pil-
lory or distract the referee (unless the ref was a *rudo*,
too), kick the good-guy *técnicos* in the balls at every
opportunity to cheat, and otherwise represent evil tri-
umphant in the squared circle.

"Ah," said Atrocidad, pleasured by the memory.
"That was when we took the belt from La Aureola,

Flecha de Jalisco, and Caballero del Espacio." La
Aureola—Golden Halo—was a religious-themed good
guy whose big gimmick was to kneel in the center of
the ring when things looked blackest, asking God to
intervene with divine righteousness. Usually that was
when he got stomped down, at which point the audience would go berserk, lofting garbage and plastic
cups of piss into the ring at the injustice of it all, per-
mitting the Halo to bounce back with his own special
brand of retributive resurrection. There is no more
perfect example of the passion play than lucha libre
wrestling, and the masked strongmen, good or bad,
were the closest thing the culture had to actual heroes
who could been seen striding the streets. Anyone
mocking the sport as precious fakery would not last
twenty seconds in a ring with one of these grapplers,
who knew the difference between reality and theatre
and did everything they could to erase the line.

Half-hour bouts featuring constant acrobatic movement quickly taught you a lot about your own personal
energies, and luchadors did it every week, risking their
lumbar support for peanuts.

El Atrocidad had wrestled championships all over
the globe, including California, from Orange County
swap meets to big-ticket bouts at the Los Angeles Sports
Arena, nearly all them as an illegal alien.

"We know this promoter in Orange County," he
said. "We fly or drive to Tijuana, usually three or four
of us, and his wife picks us up. She's totally white, hot,
a blonde, Irish, I think. The border guards see her in a
car with a bunch of Mexicans in suits, and they always
wave her through. We go up to O.C., do some bouts,
make a few hundred, have dinner, get laid a lot, then

come back, sometimes individually, sometimes as a group, but that part is easy—nobody smuggles anything *into* Mexico."

"I think they can help you," said Mano. "I think they can help you get to where you need to go."

"This bullshit…" Atrocidad indicated the empty doorway to Barney's room, meaning the killer that had filled it less than twelve hours earlier, and in a larger sense, disgust at the pervasive all-around injustice. "Mano is in danger too. We have to get you out of here. I respect Mano, and I trust you because I trust him." He shrugged. Easy. "Do you think you can make it?"

"I have to," Barney said. "Don't I?"

"I once watched El Cholo wrestle with the flu in Guadalajara. He had a 103-degree fever and we practically had to carry him to the ring. The fight starts, *tres caidas*, something like twenty minutes nonstop, and he *jumps* into the ring off the rope, doesn't miss a hold or fall, gets his ass kicked but he was supposed to that night, and before he steps out of the ring he does this little victory jump on each side, making sure he doesn't miss anybody in the audience, and they love him, because he's like defeated, right, but never broken. Then he steps out of the ring and boom, all at once, he's half-dead again."

"But he made it," said Barney.

"*Exactamente.*"

"He's very strong," said Mano of Barney. "They cut him, they shot him, he was in the Rio Satanas and did not die."

"We get him one of those big hoodie coats," said Atrocidad. "Put him in the back of the van, he keeps his hands in his pockets…it should be okay."

"If I don't bust open and start leaking at the border crossing," said Barney.

"You can walk, right?"

"Just barely. Enough to fake it."

"You have to be a pretty good liar, basically," said the wrestler, indicating that this was not only a deep virtue, but often a matter of sheer survival.

"He can walk," said Mano. "Not run, but walk, *sí*."

"You come down here to see us fight at Arena Coliseo, eh?" said Atrocidad, with just a microscopic preen.

"Yeah, I used to." Then, ruefully: "I love Mexico."

"But you have not come for a while, and when you return, it was for the wrong reason, *correcto*?"

"Yeah."

"Come back to Mexico for the right reason," said Atrocidad. "You will always have family here. But first, let us deal with the things that threaten that family. You have family, back up north?"

"No."

"Sometimes the people to whom you are bound by blood are less important than those to whom you are bound by *éticas*, by honor, yes? But sometimes, you give up your blood, you are bound to a new *familia*, maybe one you are worthy of, or one that is worthy of your honor and respect." He recited this as though it was his personal gospel. "You understand?"

"*Sí, claro*," said Barney. "Painfully."

"*Con mucho dolor*, eh?" El Atrocidad laughed raucously, his trademark evil badguy chuckle, exposing gold-rimmed teeth. He would have slapped Barney on the shoulder had he not been afraid of breaking him. "It's good for you, pain, sometimes, eh?"

"God, don't say that."

"It's true. *Es verdad*. Sometimes it is the only truth there is."

In a world of lies, Barney had to admit that the big guy was right.

There were no words with which Barney could take leave of Mano; the little puppet-like man had saved his life, risked his own.

Mano held up a highly-polished piece of river agate in a pewter setting, scarlet, alabaster, deep green, with an eyelet for a leather thong. It caught the sunlight.

"This has no value," he said. "It is a common stone. But *es muy bonita*, yes?"

"Very beautiful," said Barney, reluctant to accept it because he could not hold it in his bandaged hands. The gauze had been modified to free his working fingers, but every movement brought stabbing agony to his hands as a whole.

Mano draped the totem around Barney's neck.

"Remember me, my friend," he said.

It sufficed, for what Barney could not articulate. Finally, he said, "I'll see you again." It was all he could offer, but it was enough.

El Atrocidad's chariot was a yacht-sized Cadillac in patchy, oxidizing gold, with enfeebled rocker panels and no air conditioning. Barney was packed into the back seat between two very wide luchadors, with a third riding shotgun as Atrocidad drove them to the airport, at dismaying speed, as though piloting a Jeep through a minefield during an air raid.

Offstage, *rudos* and *técnicos* frequently hung together, or wolfed down heart-attack-sized *tortas* at the Café Cuadrilatero, a wrestling-themed eatery in Mexico

City run by another legend, Super Astro. Bitter enemies in the ring dined together after bouts; trophies
and captured masks adorned the walls. In the myth-
ology of lucha libre, a good guy could become a bad
guy in an instant, or the reverse; lose his dignity in a
hair match, regain it with a "turn" or switch in loyalties.
The cosmic balances of the universe had determined
that Barney would be ferried north by an entourage of
two good guys, two bad.

No time to stop for a Super Gladiador at Astro's,
unfortunately. One of those monstrous sandwiches
could feed about eight people...or two luchadors.

To Barney's right was Medico Odio, Dr. Hate, who
without his *máscara* resembled a burly nightclub comic
—acres of grin, big square head tattooed with scar
tissue from all the times he had bladed in the ring,
abundant *mustachio*, like Central Casting's idea of
Pancho Villa, fifty percent bigger and louder. All of the
OC-bound crew were traveling incognito, maskless.
To let Barney see them and know who they were
in civilian life was in itself a trust not to be breached,
and its name was kayfabe—not a Mexican word, pro-
nounced *K-fayb*.

You never outed a luchador; either by exposing his
true identity or yakking about the rehearsed drama
and cooperative elements of the sport. Breaking kayfabe was the worst kind of gaffe, and grounds for total
ostracization and pariah status. The term itself was
never uttered outside of the wrestling or carny indus-
tries until the 1990s, when it was hijacked by hip
know-nothings to connote insider status, and grossly
flaunted by Americans tone-deaf to mythic power.

The gold standard of Mexican wrestlers, the world-famous Hijo del Santo, scion of the legendary *Enmás-carada de Plata*, was so devoted to maintaining kayfabe that he was known to travel separately from his crew and peers, especially inside of Mexico, in order to avoid the chance that anyone might glimpse his real face when he had to do things like clear passport scrutiny.

To Barney's left was Flecha de Jalisco, a *tapatío* from Guadalajara, capital city of the state for which many wrestlers had named themselves, the most famous being Rayo de Jalisco and all his sub-named *hijos* and juniors, a whole multigenerational wrestling dynasty. His real name was Cristobal Campos Soriano; the *flecha* meant "arrow." He was the oldest fighter in the car at fifty-five and, barring a crippling accident, would be doing suicide moonsaults for another ten years. Repeated hits in the throat and a lifetime smoking habit had given him a resonant radio announcer's voice. He could speak almost sub-audibly and still be heard over the din of a crowd, without a microphone.

Up front on the right, working his way through the third of many cans of Tecate stashed in a ice cooler, was Mega Poseidon, who had gotten his gimmick, trident and all, from watching *Jason & the Argonauts* as a child, but usually worked in a fish-man monster mask of green and gold, with costume to match. He had dyed blond hair black at the roots and shorn to a military-style brush cut. His almost Brazilian eyes were that mesmerizing aqua color, very calm but somehow alien in his swarthy face.

Poseidon handed Barney's newest passport back to him. It was a first-rate job of speed forgery and would pass muster in any American scanner.

"Wow," said Barney. He was learning the clumsy

dance using his remaining fingers and thumb as a kind
of grasping tool, an unsubtle crab-claw, and was able
to dunk the passport into his coat pocket on the first
try. "Who do we owe for tickets?"

"We all got e-tickets," said Flecha. "Taken care of
by Tuntun, our homeboy in Orange County. The passport gets you through the computer, *no problemo*."

Dr. Hate made a joke about Barney's stealth status
being the grandest kayfabe of them all.

"Yeah, you need a luchador identity," said El Atrocidad with a half-smirk. "In case somebody asks us
who the hell you are."

Thus ensued a long exploration into Barney's attributes—if any could be said to apply to lucha libre—
resulting in handles mostly cut from whole cloth
anyway: first the dirty one (*Chupacabrón*), then the
ridiculous one (*Cangrejo Tres Mil*, due to the crab-
claw joke), then one that perversely fit: *El Destructor
Blanco*, the White Destroyer.

Insofar as he could grip anything, Barney gripped
the pill vials in his pockets and tried not to sweat the
rest of his life out through his pores. These hale and
belligerent men were doing their best to keep his
spirits up, to infuse him with their infectious energy.
He hoped he would not have to hang between two of
them and pretend to walk, like a marionette on
downers. When they debarked at the airport, he saw
how farcical this would be: El Atrocidad and Flecha
towered over him, while Dr. Hate and Mega-Poseidon
were each a foot shorter.

Barney tried to remember how recently he had
arrived at Benito Juárez International, Mexico's largest
air hub. Weeks or months? He had no baggage but

with the number of gear trollies the luchadors were pulling, that really didn't matter. He'd had to leave the assassin's pistol with Mano and felt naked without it, even if he was incapable of bringing it into play. The usual security, cops and soldiers were toting auto machine guns everywhere, but the 'port had remained unrattled in the post-9/11 world. Besides, they were just jumping up to Tijuana, and luchadors have a quiet way of exuding a forcefield of celebrity even when they are traveling as civilians. It is okay to sense they are wrestlers because nobody knows which wrestlers they might or might not be, and strangers defer to the most tempting choice. They got smiles of acknowledgement even from the guards as they passed, and Barney was just another one of them. Hurt in the ring, no doubt.

The hoodie coat Barney was wearing concealed a multitude of sins, but ventilation was not one of its virtues. Mummified in bandages beneath, he was starting to bake. Soon he would smell delicious.

On the plane, Dr. Hate had to help him sip a soft drink through a straw. Barney had never felt more completely helpless. He knew the air trip was partially due to his condition, since the 800-mile drive to Tijuana from Mexico City would have wrecked him. More unknown benefactors to thank.

The Tijuana airport was commonly referred to as "Rodriguez"; it had been named after some military general. The wrestlers helped Barney navigate through a tediously long bathroom stopover, got more medication inside of him, then dragged him forth to meet Valry Ayala, their blonde-headed Trojan Horse-mistress.

Valry was a lean six feet tall in flats, and even dressed

down to denim and sweatshirt she looked like a zillion
bucks in bullion. Everybody hugged her as they took
turns holding Barney up. Her smile was a little horsy
—big teeth and a little too much exposed gumline—
but her hair and eyes were classic, curly ash-blonde
and penetrating green, like a Heineken bottle with a
light behind it. Nice back porch and healthy natural
breasts, yearning to run free. She switched her hips
when she walked. It was no accident.

"So you're our special guest star," she said to Barney,
jamming out a hand.

Barney held up one of his bandaged mitts. "Sorry."

"No worries," she said cheerfully, touching his damaged face with long, lacquered nails. "We'll fix ya up."

Tuntun Ayala was a fixture in the low-budget Orange
County wrestling circuit, catering to Southern California's bustling Latino populace. At various times he
had wrestled as Jayson xXx, Ice Dragon, Sirial Killer,
High Voltage and Deathmaster 2, and had at least
twelve other rotating identities on his resume. He and
his tribe organized the shows, carting a portable ring
setup all over L.A. County, and he worked in Mexico
as often as he "unofficially imported" the talent that
locals wanted to see. Through several previous wives
he had begotten his own generation of future ring
workers and then met Valry during a televised match,
right before the collapse of *Canal Vente-Dos*, Los
Angeles' Channel 22, which lost most of its analog-
broadcast Hispanic programming to cable. Once Tuntun
zeroed his sights on Valry and went blonde-blind,
his then-current marriage was swiftly and completely
doomed.

Marrying a beautiful white chick had definite sociopolitical advantages, and she was the best den mother Tuntun could have wished for. The trip back across the border went exactly as El Atrocidad had said it would.

Barney was back in the U.S.A.

But the largesse did not stop there. Tuntun, who turned out to be a blustery, dark-skinned giant with cornrowed black hair, insisted on seeing to Barney's comfort and taking him the extra hour or so north on the 101 to Los Angeles personally.

Typically, Barney had to promise to see everyone again—unwanted connective tissue that was not in his nature. He had no idea how to even begin paying these people back, or what to pay them with. He was stony. Moreover, he got the idea that to fob them off with money would constitute an insult. Mostly, he kept quiet and grateful.

In an astonishingly short period of time, less than a day, he had gone from being marooned in the middle of Mexico to dictating fill-out forms for hospital check-in. Tuntun did all the writing. Bed, board, doctors, nurses, beeping machines, and best of all, brand-name sedatives.

The crew dispensed their hearty goodbyes and begged off—they had work to do and matches to fight.

Barney drifted off to uncomplicated sleep on a real bed, clean linens, the clamor of demons inside his skull gradually receding.

Nobody was more surprised than him when he awoke and found himself staring at his old buddy, Armand, in a bed in the same ward.

Lather, rinse, repeat.

°

First the hostage hotel, then Mano's home, then the *clinica*, and now a modern hospital in an American city. The fourth Bleeding Room in which Barney found himself washed ashore was arguably the most painful, as they continually drugged him and hauled his ass to and fro to remove bullets, drain infections, resocket his shoulder, bind his ribs, flush his metabolism, and otherwise get him back to zero.

A wadcutter is a flat-nosed bullet about as aerodynamic as a clinker brick, which tumbles to inflict maximum carnage on delivery. Sucio had shot Barney with four of them. But his aim had been totally *bandido*, more for show than efficiency, and Barney had miraculously slipped by on the curve.

He had picked up an intestinal parasite in the Rio Satanas; no surprise there.

He had been fast asleep the first time his friend Karlov had visited, to deliver a new Ruger .44 to Armand for his inspection and approval. Armand was packing heat in a hospital; you had to laugh.

Armand looked starved and shrunken in a humid hospital jonnie. Normally swarthy and piratical of eye, his glint was diminished and he seemed pale. He didn't rise from his bed.

"What the hell happened to you?" Barney croaked. His throat was arid, his vision blurry. He felt doped and bulky, as though inflated to twice his rated capacity.

"My appendix," Armand said. "Bastard up and quit on me."

Armand had nothing but recovery time to listen to Barney's story. He was stuck in the hospital for at least another four days, under observation to see that he did not blow a major hose in the aftermath of the unanticipated appendectomy that had landed him, by purest chance, in the bed next to Barney's.

Something Armand told him in response to his story stuck in the filter of Barney's mind:

"What happened to *you*…that was pure gringo."

There was a truth in there, and Barney could see it now. His distress had not issued from Mexican sadists, rough-riding a displaced *gabacho*. It had come as a result of respectable Americans acting less than respectable, as many do when your back is turned.

"They took something of mine, Armand. And I want to get it back."

When Barney said that, he was not talking about his amputated fingers. He showed Armand the mutilations merely to slam the point home.

Armand laughed. "*Look* at us, man." It was pretty silly. Then he let out a long, contemplative sigh, and said, "So what do you want to do?"

Barney stretched his neck back against the pillows and felt a vertebra pop with relief. "I'm working on that. But first I want to find out who the best sports surgeon is in this place."

That turned out to be Dr. Matthew Brandywine, an orthopedist who specialized in hand surgery. When Barney told him what he wanted, the doctor immediately expressed doubts, but it was already too late—Barney had put the glint of a challenge in the good doctor's eye. In that moment, it was all over except for a ton of releases and indemnifications.

Karlov broke the news that Barney's apartment had been cleaned out and re-rented. It was no palace anyway, just a way station, a sleeping berth for the little time Barney did not spend at the shooting range, which is where most of his valuables were secure under lock and key—firearms, cash, assorted ID. He did not keep photographs. His quarters had always been rather Spartan and he was disinterested in television, popular music, the Internet. Politics, religion and mass culture held no appeal. What he enjoyed was keeping his profile below the radar of the ordinary world. After Iraq he had done a few gigs for subterranean figures who offered good money, which is how he had come to meet the Old Assassin. There were no relatives, no encumbrances. He had enjoyed the company of women from time to time, but only until he could feel the cement hardening around his ankles. He possessed very few legitimate documents of any relevance. Not one to horde his past, Barney found the past had a nasty habit of finding you when it wanted to complicate your current life.

As it had with Carl, for painful example.

Karlov had rescued Barney's fish, of course, because Armand had been charged with its care. That was how unspoken duty worked. People like Karlov and Armand were part of the reason Barney had never needed contractually obligated friends.

Christoph Ivan Karlov had come to America after the fall of the Berlin Wall. Having functioned at various times as weapons master for KGB cells and the former Soviet military, Karlov found in America a vast new horizon of firearms to modify, tinker with, improve or restore, particularly for gun collectors obsessed by the pristine or victimized by wily forgers. The tides of shifting jobs in a free market economy had deposited him on the shores of Los Angeles, where he had become the beneficiary of a large number of serious firearms enthusiasts with a lot of discretionary income.

His lush hair had been white since his twenty-third birthday. He personally installed his corrective lenses into stainless steel shooter's frames, and since he was a bit chipmunk-cheeked, the specs always appeared to be squeezing his head at the temples. If he was your audience, he tended to stare for long periods of time without blinking, less rudeness than a measure of the concentration he accorded you. Generally he was silent, contemplative, almost scary in his focus, infinitely patient, and knew more information about more guns than any ten other people Barney could name.

Armand Arnott, by contrast, was hale and jokey. He occasionally got loud when he drank too much; he could be over-reactive when provoked, a steamroller who would not quit and would not back down, and absolutely the kind of man you would want at your back in a crisis. Loyalty was an almost Sicilian thing with him, and he cursed under his breath a great deal when Barney related, in fits and starts, the tale of what had befallen him in Mexico. Armand practiced regularly at the range where Barney worked, and routinely captured gold at shooting competitions, where he favored handguns he could wield with sniper precision—Barney had once seen him shoot the eye out of a jack of spades at nearly sixty yards with no optics.

"How's the fish?" said Barney.

"Swimming. Pooping. Doing fish things." Karlov folded his hands and sat down after ruffling his snow-white hair, the *cleanest* hair Barney had ever seen. "I think the fish, he likes watching my television."

Barney thanked him unnecessarily, for taking care of things in his absence, and picking up the ball after Armand's incapacitation.

"Well now, this here looks like a meeting of some

kind of terrorist organization for sure," came a booming
voice from the corridor as Sirius Johnson made his
entrance. Ex-LAPD, currently diversified into public
relations, Sirius was the guy who most often organized
shooting excursions for this quartet, or the occasional
poker night, bowling, dinner, or other diversions to
space out their serious trigger time. He was also the
man who could help you finesse a concealed carry
permit, if you needed such a thing in the state of
California. His heavy eyelids lent him a sleepy aspect,
but beyond was a gaze of pure espresso that missed
very little. He had recently started getting artful with
his razor, sculpting a complicated beard-moustache-
sideburn frame for his round face that looked like it
took a lot of maintenance. Not quite vain enough to
shave his head against encroaching pattern baldness,
Sirius had compromised at a quarter-inch trimmer chop.

Like Barney, these men moved between the spaces
of the ordinary world of people. It would be useless to
call them by race, profile, or statistics, because you
walk past them every day and don't notice them. Who
was taller, shorter, older or younger, it didn't matter.
Their names, like Barney's, were fluid things, adapt-
able at a moment's notice to new identities, stealth
personae.

Appraising the wreckage that used to be Barney,
Sirius arched a brow and said, "So…enjoy your trip?"

"I lost my apartment," Barney said. "Karlov collected
my stuff, but if I ever get out of here, I'm officially
homeless."

It seemed as though America did not want Barney
back, either. His home, such as it was, had been assim-
ilated. He assured everyone present that he could stay
at the range, had done so many times. There was room,

comfort and familiarity there. He had not really lost anything. Except.

"I'm glad you guys are all here, so I only have to tell the story once. I've told Armand a little bit of it, but I'll give you the definitive version, gory details and all. There's a reason I'm doing this, and I'll tell you up-front that I am in full possession of my senses, so don't blame my meds. When I get done telling the story, I have a proposition for you, but it's not really something I can ask of any of you. I think I know you all well enough to risk putting these ideas out into the air, and if I'm full of shit, tell me. As far as you're concerned, this is just a made-up story about an imaginary guy named Barney, and what happened to him. Armand's been asking me what I think I want to do after this, and I've been mulling it over—asleep, not asleep, coming at it from every angle I can think of. Here's what I want to do: I want to tell you the story. And if, at the end of the story, what I have to say sounds insane to any of you, don't say yes, don't say no, no buts or maybes…just get up and walk out of the room if you're not down. Fair enough?"

Sirius hauled in an extra chair. Barney recounted everything he could remember. And then he told the three men what he wanted to do.

Nobody left.

Barney barely saw the fifth Bleeding Room thanks to the benefits of modern anesthesia. His body first had to be strong and adjudged fit enough to withstand the rigors of induced unconsciousness, and there was no way the dual procedure could be performed by Dr. Brandywine with a local.

More forms. More time.

Barney's hands were butterflied like lamb shanks so
Dr. Brandywine could get at the interstitial bones—
the ones no longer required due to the missing-in-
action index fingers—and remove them. Resectioning
to close up the gaps. Nerves and blood vessels were
reconnected with microfilament too small to see with
the naked eye. Bones never meant to be neighbors
were brazed together. The remaining healthy skin now
gave enough surplus to fold closed and suture. They
would leave very interesting scar patterns. The shortest
of these multiple surgeries was a ten-hour stretch.

Add plasma, antibiotics, painkillers. Mix well and
let set.

Serves one.

The result was an adequately proportioned, though
decidedly bizarre-looking three fingered hand so natural
in shape that your eye was deceived into wondering
what was amiss at first view. It was something you had
to devote time to noticing. Freakish, maybe; odd, yes.
Barney was re-evolving from near-useless flippers to a
tri-taloned Martian hand from *War of the Worlds*, or
what Mickey Mouse actually hid beneath that three-
fingered glove.

But no bump, no stub, no disproportion.

Now all he had to do was learn to work with these
new tools.

A finger stump would have necessitated special
handgrip grooving for stabilization. The stretch of
hand minus a finger would have to be accommodated
by an extended handgrip, and the trigger, modified for
a middle finger wrap—the middle finger was almost a
whole knuckle too much for a proper pull. Gross gun
weight, and therefore felt recoil, would have to be factored into the smaller overall palm area.

Karlov was working out that problem right now, somewhere else, leaning over a gun bench, probably wearing his double-magnifying specs for close work. Concocting new mutant forms of firearm. Making them evolve.

Armand was dealing with ballistics—what kind of rounds, how many grains of powder per cartridge, range, kick, bullet type. The swage die was his al-chemical furnace. He had always manufactured his own ammo.

Sirius commenced a round of interviews with Barney that led to a pile of pencil sketches in slow layers of accumulation. It was all about strategy. Penetration routes, exit schema, logistics. Drills on backups, back-stops, Plan Bs, contingencies. Who, what, and how many. Room plans. Terrain. Things that could not be recalled or anticipated had to be imagined. Best guesses. Smartest options.

Barney commenced therapy on both hands as soon as the seams set and they were sure not to burst under stress like wet piñatas. Squeezing, lifting, isometrics in an agonizingly slow but progress-oriented crawl.

The first red-letter day came when Barney could cycle the trigger on Armand's Magnum through one complete double-action pull. Snap.

Thirty-nine to go.

For nearly a month and a half both his hands were imprisoned in nylon cross-lace braces with metal sup-ports, like corsets for his wrists.

Red-letter day Number Two saw Barney feeding himself without a drop of spillage. His fingers and thumbs were beginning to get to know each other again.

Karlov brought him a rebalanced SIG Super .40

with a whisper trigger; Barney managed five pulls.

Which hung him up for another week when his hands started to bleed.

Barney's goldfish croaked eight days after he set up housekeeping at the gun range, with the benediction of owner/manager Neil Takami, who secretly appreciated the extra nighttime security. Barney awoke to find the fish floating sideways, dead as roadkill, nobody's fault, these things just happen sometimes. Following a brief unspoken encomium, Barney gave his late fish a burial at sea with honors, if you stop to consider that every sewer pipe and outflow system in Los Angeles eventually empties into the Pacific Ocean.

Barney had never watched television while on his own. He had watched the fish. From what he had gleaned of television while immobilized in the hospital—at least, the noisy and idiotic programs Armand subjected him to during their mutual convalescence— he wasn't missing a thing of worth. Mano had not had a TV, either, and Barney didn't have one here.

This left Barney with nothing much to do when he was by himself, surrounded by armament he was incapable of utilizing professionally, and amateurism grated his psyche. He hung with his crew: Karlov, refining his modifications to a variety of firearms; Armand, checking in to test his latest cartridges; Sirius, to pursue an overall mission objective. It was Barney that was the albatross here, his slow healing, crippled movement and nearly insurmountable pain deftly yoking an anvil to any concept of forward motion.

These were the classic ingredients for genuine despair.

He could head-butt the pain. He had to; there were

three more operations on his hands after the first one, and each of those came with mandated recovery periods with too much time spent awake and luridly aware of the pulsing of blood through throbbing fingers, even the ghost fingers.

He could rationalize the slow-motion of healing. At least it was goal-oriented.

He could become a fast-food zombie, staring glassy-eyed at a TV until his brains dribbled out his ear. No, scratch that.

He could discover or innovate adapted forms of movement to replace outmoded or restricted ones. That was forward-thinking and resourceful.

But he could not beat the sulfurous ebony cloud that swaddled his emotions, because that was the area in which Barney was least prepared for combat. He had kissed the despair in Mexico—sideswiped it— then had head-butted the emotion while imprisoned, but it had never loomed as skin-crawlingly imminent as it did now, when he was supposedly free. He saw himself as a drained vessel of exhausted resources, no surplus tanks, running on the memory of fumes. His bodily energies had been sunk into tissue regeneration and the mass production of antibodies and white cells. His brain felt as if it had been dry-cleaned, sandblasted and re-shelved, empty.

Even as mundane an activity as going to the market— once he could locomote—seemed off-kilter to Barney, as though he had rematerialized in a parallel world and was faking his way through the most ordinary moves so the natives wouldn't notice and lynch him for being an outsider. He developed a fondness for an energy drink called Primer Pop, but apart from that and the booze in his miniature fridge at the gun range, he had seemingly lost the ability to discern foodstuffs. He generally ate with his crew, or ate something they bagged along. He found himself standing in an overlit aisle, his ears assaulted by Beatles muzak, unable to determine exactly which flavor of Ape-Os cereal to buy. Orangutan flavor? Gorilla Granola? It was as though some essential program in his head had been deleted.

He had to fill himself back up with something, and all he had was a dormant vein of raw hatred.

They took Erica; they got her, man, grabbed her ass right out from under me, I haven't got a pot to piss in…there's nobody else I can trust in a shitstorm like this…will you help me?

It was an art, that kind of simulated feeling. Hysteria helped sell the mark. The best users always advantaged a ticking clock and ego—help is needed *now*; you are the only candidate, and a yes vote means they've just hooked their latest sucker. Your utility was the outer limit of friendship.

In Iraq, Carl had performed a long spiel about who might live and who might die and who might keep in touch, after. About the kind of friends you don't see for years, then pick up right where you left off. That had sounded warm and inviting, all right, an ideal to wish for in the face of daily death. But—all cards down—it was about using people.

Carl was usable, so Felix Rainer had used him. Erica had probably played them both. Wasn't that how the food chain worked? The big ones got eaten by the bigger ones, who got gobbled up by the biggest ones, and it didn't matter how big or bad you were, there was always some carnivore bigger or badder. If they couldn't make you chum, then they made you a chump. True predators could whiff this vulnerability with a surety that gilded their genes all the way back to caveman days. The ground rule of predation: eat instead of being eaten.

The theory of the mark was that you invited usury by being too eager, greedy, gullible, or all three. Barney's ego image of himself as fixer for the halt and clueless had doomed him.

You had to not care about anything. Sacrifice anyone. Scoot with no baggage. And keep breathing—that was the end that justified any means.

One trick of psychology was to disempower your tormentors. That mate of yours who fucked you over? Think of them as decayed, diseased, repulsive. Stop tacitly forgiving them and go on the offensive. Barney realized with an acidic jolt that he was still cutting slack for Carl Ledbetter based on events of years past. Carl was not that guy now. He had to be a new guy, somebody Barney could despise enough to kill.

As for the repulsive part, well, Barney had worn that suit already. It wasn't his, didn't fit him, and wasn't it time to pass it on to somebody who really deserved it?

He could be like the Old Assassin, immune to feeling, his emotions shut down and turned off, all human sympathy on mute. Or he could be like he was now, a victim, a mark, a schmuck. There had to be another option, a middle ground, and Barney found its boundaries when he allowed himself the luxury of pure hate, unadulterated by self-pity or misplaced notions of fairness.

It took ten months before he felt as whole again as he was going to be for the rest of his life. By that time he had reconnected with the art of the true gunman. He had re-learned everything, traveling back beyond novice to start as virgin. The grip, the stance, targeting accurately, knowing your loads, sensing how many rounds remained from the weight of the firearm in your hand, it was all an uphill climb on a mountain of shit, hoping that when you found the single rose at the summit, you hadn't lost the sense of smell.

It was a rebirth.

Newly born, Barney found that only the hatred had endured, and now it was purer than ever.

Part Three
Gun Work

"Now, this here is a beauty for close-ups," said Karlov. With a showman's flourish he displayed a Smith & Wesson revolver with an eight-inch barrel. From the side it looked like a real hand cannon.

"Twenty-two caliber, ten-round cylinder, the trigger is a feather and it shoots like a horny teenager. No kick at all."

Superior caliber did not always mean bigger, fatter bullets. With a .22, you could put all ten rounds into someone without killing them, and usually by round five they would tell you whatever you wanted to know. It was all in the application.

"Moving to slightly larger armament…" Karlov opened his jacket to reveal a complicated web holster of his own design. It held four pistols, two on each side, revolvers on top, semi-autos below. He enumerated the guns: "A .357 Magnum…Super .40…9-mil….45. The spine rack holds three mags each for the semi-autos. Speed loaders for the revolvers up here."

"Damn," said Armand, stroking his chin.

"Body armor," said Sirius, laying out what looked like a floppy, lime-green wetsuit top on the gun range counter. "Standard Kevlar is comprised of thirty or forty layers of synthetic fabric. It's bulky and restricts movement. This is some new shit they came up with for the Army."

"The liquid armor?" said Armand.

"Yeah. This is a sandwich of Kevlar fabric encasing a polymer infused with nanobits of silica. Basically, polyethylene glycol and purified sand. It's called 'sheer thickening liquid' and it stiffens instantaneously into a shield when hit by a bullet. It reverts to liquid state when the energy from the hit dissipates. Even a top of the line bulletproof vest can't protect you from stabbing, say, or shrapnel. This can. It's lighter, more flexible, allows maximum mobility."

Barney just whistled silently. "It's a science fiction suit," he said. "No way this is legal."

"You didn't say anything about *legal*," said Sirius with a knowing grin.

"Yeah, that's right, I didn't. Hmm."

"Let's see your hands," said Karlov to Barney, who displayed them.

The thumbs flowed toward the (former) middle fingers with a natural web of skin. Except for the fact that each hand was one digit shy, they appeared normal. When Barney made a fist, you could pick out a white webwork of scar tracks. That Dr. Brandywine wasn't an artist; he was a sorcerer.

Karlov handed him the customized .22. "Let me see your reach."

Barney extended the gun in the general direction of a paper target about forty feet downrange.

"Okay, now hold that extension for five minutes."

And the end of three hundred excruciating seconds —which Sirius had to count off individually—Karlov said, "Now do your trigger pulls."

Barney managed nineteen out of forty. His hand started to bleed and he blotted it with a paper towel.

"Thought so," said Karlov. "I have confabulated a

little assist for you." He produced a pair of one-inch-wide strips of nylon that resembled dog leashes. "Thumb hole at this end," he said. "The other end loops around your neck." He threaded Barney into the contraption and bade him hold the pistol up again. "Now, lean forward. Push with your arm as though you are stretching. You see?"

The strap provided a stable hand-arm-eye link through very gentle tension. It was like a built-in bench rest. Karlov showed Barney how to adjust the tiny buckles he had installed for a snug fit.

"How's your trigger wrap?" He was referring to the surplus reach afforded by using his middle finger to trigger.

"Feels like I've got a Vienna sausage spliced onto the end of my finger."

The next gun he handed Barney was a Beretta .92FS Brigadier in 9-millimeter. "Try this with the strap."

Barney's hand wrapped the butt and his fingertip kissed the groove of the match trigger. Karlov had replaced the commander-style hammer with a skeletonized Beretta Elite. "What did you do?"

"Machined the frame myself. Fattened the grip to make up for the distance in your finger reach. Enlarged the backstrap and made a set of palm swells out of rubber with recessed screw mounts; you can feel out the different sizes and pick what feels natural for you. A four-pound pull in single action. Made the slide heavier. There was too much trigger travel so I put in a speedbump. I think it's beefy, but the bulk should give you more control. Oh, and it will take hi-cap mags now—22 rounds."

"I'd lose those crappy sights," said Sirius. "Put some Tritium night sights on it."

"Not for close-quarter," said Karlov. "Discrimination is more important for speed shooting."

Sirius nodded. They had all seen men who could shoot faster than they could think. You spot a weapon in the hands of what you think is a hostile, your eyes zap to center mass, your finger pulls the trigger, and a round is flying before your brain catches up and informs you that you have just launched a bullet at a friendly instead of a gunner or at a hostage who turns out to be unarmed.

Armand rummaged in his bag for a rack of cartridges and loaded Barney's clip. "Shoot these and tell me what you think. One hundred and twenty-three grain, full metal jacket."

"Not hollow points?" said Barney.

"Might cause it to jam."

Armand's slugs rocketed from the muzzle at 445 foot-pounds and 1,280 feet per second. With the strap, Barney kept all his tags in the main torso grid of the target at twenty-five yards.

Most gun work took place close-up. Ninety percent of gunfights occur at distances of nine feet or less. Of that ninety percent, eighty percent happen within three feet. Amazingly, defensive shooters tended to score one shot in ten at those distances, because you had to factor in bad light, sleepiness, surprise, or compromised placement. A ten percent hit rate when you were shooting for your life was not acceptable.

"Coat those with Teflon," said Armand, "and they'll grease through a vest like butter."

"Shotguns?" said Barney.

"Full size Benelli M4 semi-autos with a stock, a pistol

grip, and a combat muzzle. Every load from buckshot
to flechettes." The M4 had originally been developed
for Marine Corps and SWAT use. Pumpguns were for
showoffs, or the movies.

"Smoke?" said Barney.

"Them smoke grenades are the only military ord
we have," said Sirius. "They're not exactly what you
wanted, but—"

"Do they *smoke*?" said Barney.

Sirius decided to put his explanation on hold. "Yeah,
they smoke just fine."

"Shipping?" said Barney.

"Already taken care of," said Sirius.

"Jesus…anybody want a pizza?" Barney was surprised at how quickly he had run out of questions.
These three men had him covered.

The reason they had thrown Barney their uncondi-
tional support was a bit dicey. They all possessed super-
lative gun expertise and none had cause to casually risk
their lives. They all had been in life-or-death situations
involving gunplay and the use of firepower. They all
had known combat, urban or wartime, usually from a
defense posture. What Barney had offered them was
the kind of opportunity that comes rarely, and is almost
never planned—a tactical assault on superior forces
where each man's knowledge and experience would
determine the outcome. No safe fallbacks and no guar-
antees. You can talk for a lifetime of conviction to
certain absolutes, but rarely do you get the chance
to purposefully acid-test those maxims in a real-world
context. This was a chance for these men to find out if
what they knew—or what they thought they knew—
was worth anything.

Frankly, Barney felt as if they had just been waiting

around all their lives for the right excuse. The crime of non-action was on par with giving a talented artist plenty of paint, brushes, canvas, inspiration, and time ...and then not allowing him to paint.

There was a wealth of wiggle time if anybody wanted to bail. Three more weeks, minimum, of working the guns on the range and warming up the newer guns through their break-in periods, usually measured in hundreds of rounds...or, in Barney's case, two to three thousand rounds per gun before he began to develop the correct muscle memory for accurate handling in combat. Each weapon had its own personality and eccentricities, and familiarization was essential. Each weapon had its brothers and sisters, multiples of Karlov's painstaking labor, and they all had to be broken in.

A lot of bang-bang, enough to make you wash the gunpowder out of your hair every night.

Training specs called for a 70/30 ratio of dry fire to live fire, with a shooting timer. Armand actually video-taped Barney's range drills; tape doesn't lie.

Before it settled into enough of a routine to make them lazy, Barney announced that he was taking a little trip, by himself.

Sirius was a tiny bit disappointed, since he had worked out labyrinthine plans for interstate firearms transport; there were the complications of multiple IDs for all them at various altitudes of impermeability, ticketing for trains and planes, proper camouflage of any potential paper (or Internet) trail, lodgings, rally points, emergency fallback rendez, and clean work cars with the right paper. All the coordination of logistics made Sirius feel like a career criminal, or a roadie for a heavy metal band.

"All this prep makes me feel like a career criminal," Sirius said. "Or a roadie for a heavy metal band."

"Hey, at least you don't have to score big flour sacks of blow," said Barney. "Or platoons of hookers."

"Or waste time cherry-picking the right color M&Ms," said Armand.

"I've got some ironclad resources here," returned Sirius. "I just don't wanna waste 'em."

"You're not," said Barney. "Just tell me who your guy is in New Jersey." He was referring to a strip yard Sirius had mentioned where he could obtain a non-descript vehicle with alternate plates, not a junker.

Barney's first port of call was New York City, a place where possession of a firearm can get you automatic jail time.

The hardest part about finding Felix Rainer in New York, for Barney, was choosing the right business suit. About half-strength Armani was what he required in order to present the correct nouveau-riche profile. The illusion only needed to fool everyone for less than a running minute of time.

The data pull on Felix Rainer was notably public. In 1995—after the junk bond boom of the 1980s and the brief last-round flurry of dotcoms in the early 1990s—he split from a liquid but undistinguished bro-kerage firm to co-found The Bleecker Street Group with two other partners. They kept the company lean as they began buying corporate properties and learned the pleasures of private equity, then of running a hedge fund specializing in distressed debt. Through calculated strikes they prospered, branching out into brand-extensions and country-specific restructuring funds...which to Barney whispered "Mexico."

On closer examination it was easy to see that Bleecker Street's maverick risk structure was pretty kissin' close to gambling, buying chemical companies out of favor in 2004 and taking them public in foreign countries when the old-economy names got hot again. Your best opportunities to sock away millions came when legitimate banks were willing to provide lender leverage into the billions. They acquired and unloaded office buildings faster than playing lightning Monopoly, and were always raising capital for their latest buyout fund.

Rainer was low-profile, hewing to the maxim laid down by Wall Street superstar Aldous Blackmoor: "Never be the poster boy. When the era changes, the poster boy gets ripped off the wall."

Rainer and his crew were Harvard hustlers, always on the sniff for Justice Department investigations into what were called "club buyouts." When quoted, they worried about interest rates; in private they amassed astonishing debt in order to bulk-purchase; Rainer's phrase for it was "economies of scale," which to Barney translated as that old TV commercial in which the screaming carpet salesman says, *How do we do it? VOLUME!*"

It took less than a day for Barney to sketch Felix Rainer's movement template. The guy began a rigorous workday at 7:30 AM sharp and went everywhere by chauffeured limousine. He owned the entire top floor of the ovoid Capitol Towers Building on Columbus Circle. Private staff and security measures had him pretty boxed, but Barney knew there was no such thing as genuine security this side of the grave.

Finding a photograph had been difficult but not impossible. Rainer was a fiftyish man with hair plugs and one of those skin-cancer sunlamp tans that looked radioactive.

Barney decided to take the guy in his limo, after business hours.

Manhattan was busy losing the last dregs of summer —warm days, cool nights. At a mid-town commercial shipping outlet Barney picked up a clad plastic case festooned with security tape and warning stickers: HIGH-SPEED PHOTOGRAPHIC FILM—EXTREMELY SENSITIVE. The interior surfaces were sheeted in lead foil and the dense, high-impact foam padding ferried Barney's work kit: a piece, several mags, cleaning kit, extra cash and alternate ID, and a coded emergency cellphone.

The gun was a solid, Nitron-finished P229 Elite in .357 SIG. Karlov liked SIGs and so did Barney. Some guys were Glock men; others swore by the myth-laden Colt, but the names were always spoken with a gravity religious people reserved for saints: Remington, Ruger, Browning, Beretta, Kimber, a whole pantheon of new gods for modern times.

SIG Sauer was proof that Germany had successfully invaded America. The "SIG" was an acronym for Swiss Industrial Company (*Schweizerische Industrie-Gesell-schaft*); the "Sauer" came from the incorporation of German gunmakers J.P. Sauer & Sohn, GmbH, of Eckernförde in the early 1970s. Nineteen eighty-five marked the rebirth of the entire assembly of companies as SIGARMS, which rapidly became a favorite of military and law enforcement during a time when cops were discovering how often they were outgunned in the street. Their handguns were devastatingly well-built and had stopping power to burn. They were also hefty—a real handful—but their actions crisp and their delivery, spot-on. They were no longer made overseas, but in New Hampshire. Barney had never been disappointed by a SIG.

This one featured a short reset trigger that eliminated "trigger slap" and made the pulls short and fast in either single or double action. Karlov had substituted Hogue wraparound grips and beefed the frame by half a pound. There was also a Safariland speed scabbard for concealed carry.

The mags contained Armand's latest concoction, his version of a 150-grain EPR, or Extreme Penetration Round, that could penetrate 20-gauge steel or most body armor.

Barney had drilled with both this gun and this ammo for a month. It could devastate a kill zone but had the kick of a .22.

His gear installed in a newly-bought attaché case, Barney caught lunch at a Greek diner, barely tasting the food but registering the mild amp of the strong coffee. The nylon steady-straps Karlov had conceived were already around his neck, the thumb loops tucked into his jacket sleeves.

He had thought briefly of wearing gloves with built-in index fingers of foam, slightly curled for a naturalistic look, until he had wandered about in the walking world for awhile and realized no one really took notice of his hands. Some time later, he might have to hide his special attributes, conceal his difference, but he did not feel that way right now. These were his hands; the world would just have to cope. His hands were him—crippled, then altered, then reborn, but still functioning. Like a clip, his hands had so many shots in them before they were exhausted.

He spent an extra day to reliably clock Felix Rainer's circuit, annotating in-times and out-times. The money-man, per an aggressive transactional profile, did not have time for lunches taken off-site. Evening functions used up 45 minutes in transit from the office to Capitol Towers, allowing for a costume change and spruce-up. Different weapons, evening-dress armament for a different brand of warfare. His chariot was a Corsair stretch that looked to Barney to be armored similarly to the limo he had driven in Mexico. He had two alternating drivers, both graduates of the school of physical threat—skintight suits over imposing bodies, packing hip holsters. The wait zone was a gated garage at Capitol, probably leading to a private elevator. Too many cameras there; too much exposure.

Okay, so it was a quitting-time date, then.

Barney had billeted himself in a mid-range hotel in the upper 50s full of foreign tourists or businessmen. Easy to blend, there. Since his credit card was imaginary, that bill did not matter. He could have watched all the cable porn he wanted. Content did not interest him but he did keep the TV on, volume dialed almost to zero, for the duration of his stay. It was another presence in the room and a harmless one, something he had keenly missed in Mexico, where another presence usually signaled yet another beating.

During off hours, Rainer's limo enjoyed a special curbside yellow zone on West 58th Street near Eighth Avenue, probably with the sanction of bribed cops. While on duty it circulated around the business

district; Rainer's office was spitting distance from the
World Trade Center site. If it parked, it had itself a
hide and Barney never spotted it. The driver never
seemed to take a meal or bathroom break, and he only
left the vehicle to watchdog Rainer in person. The
afternoon of the second day was spent tracking the
limo's ups and downs in the city, so Barney had found
the car connection provided by Sirius to be useful,
although he hated driving in Manhattan traffic as much
as any sane person would.

Barney never stopped to ask himself if he was crazy.
Any more than Rainer and lunch, he didn't have the
time.

This was going to have to go fast.

Within fifteen seconds of the limousine curbing in
front of the skyscraper housing the Bleecker Street
Group, at precisely 7:35 in the evening, Barney
strolled up to the driver's side door with his free hand
grasping a shield wallet designating him as a New York
City detective. He made the familiar hand-rolling
motion and the driver, an enormous bodybuilder in
livery, buzzed the window down and regarded him
impatiently.

Barney stuck the SIG right into his ear canal. The
chauffeur's movements were restricted by the door,
his seat belt, and the general fact that he tended to fill
the entire driver's space.

"Scoot over," said Barney.

"Awww…*shit*," said the driver, resigned.

Barney took note of the obvious bulge of gun saddle
on the man's right hip. He was a southpaw. Once they
were safe and cozy behind tinted windows, Barney
said, "Gun. Take it out, right hand, two fingers on the

butt. Go on, belt yourself in. Good. Now sit on your hands, palms down. Good."

The driver rolled his eyes, torqued at being blind-sided, knowing this would reflect badly on his rating. "What the fuck you want, man?"

"I want you to keep doing what I tell you."

The driver's gun was a simple Browning Hi-Power in nine millimeter, no jazz. Barney quickly found a backup piece in a drop door under the dashboard—a polymer-framed Cobra Patriot, also in nine. He hooked them through the open privacy divider into the cabin of the limo.

The driver did not have an ankle gun. He was not packing cuffs, a stun gun or a telescoping baton. Too much gear for the fit of his suit. About all he carried besides a wallet was his personal cellphone, which was in a slot on the dash. Barney popped the battery and chip and tossed that, too.

Barney quickly located the driver's side "panic button" transmitter and disabled it. Then he neutral-ized the car phone.

"Fuck, dude, you gonna cost me my job, you know that."

"No I'm not," said Barney, scanning the perimeter. "Question One: Is he armed?"

The driver knew the advantages of all-business when facing down a gun. "No sir. He never carries a weapon. He voted for that asshole Schumer—"

"Pay attention," said Barney, keeping him on track. "Question Two: How long?"

"Five minutes tops, from when he beeps me, sir."

"Stop calling me sir. That leaves us about a minute and a half. What's your name?"

The guy looked around as though he'd just taken a bite of pizza and lost a pepperoni in his clothes. "Uh, Malcolm, sir…I mean, Malcolm."

"Okay, Malcolm. The man who pays your salary is a piece of shit, a Wall Street player who damned near got me perished. Play this wrong and *you* perish, my friend. You perish first. The slugs in this gun will go through anything you can get behind, and if you fuck me, you won't be able to take cover fast enough, because I'm pissed off, and you don't want me pissed off at you instead of your boss. You copy?"

Malcolm nodded, a single up-down head bob. "I have to get out of the car to—"

"No you don't," said Barney. "Let him be irritated. He's always in a hurry, am I right?"

"Generally." A massive sigh escaped the big man. "Shit…he gets in half the time by himself, anyway, unless there's, y'know, somebody with him."

"Somebody with him today?"

"No, sir. Dinner at Le Cercle Rouge at eight-thirty. He's meeting people there."

"Well, he's going to be a tot late, I think."

Felix Rainer, positive match on the photo, exited the revolving doors across a tiled promenade and bee-lined for the limousine.

"Okay, Malcolm, it's shit-or-git time. You run and your boss is dead for sure, and so are you—I'll make sure you're first. You drive and do as you're told and we all walk away. You try anything fancy—erratic driving, speeding, anything out of the ordinary trip back up to Capitol Towers—and I'll put two in your back and one in your brain pan, right through the divider. You are to keep both hands on the wheel.

Pretend they're glued there. You move them off the wheel, and you catch three. You wink funny at the next car at a stoplight, and you catch three. You got all that?"

Malcolm nodded.

Before Malcolm could slip his shoulder harness, Barney was out of the driver's side door and making a quick scuttle for the back of the limo—inelegant, but necessary since Barney knew on approach the rear doors would be locked until needed. Felix Rainer could not see a thing over the roof of the car. Barney knew Malcolm's impulse would be to bolt, to dive out the passenger side, to telegraph some kind of warning, and it would take him a couple of seconds to figure it out and act in favor of his continued survival. Before Malcolm could fully resume the pilot position, Barney was slotted into the upper starboard corner of the cabin, where he could keep an eye on both driver and passenger. He swept the scattered cellphone parts and Malcolm's guns into a bar cabinet just as Rainer opened his own door and climbed inside, oblivious, impervious to any drama other than his own.

"Malcolm, goddammit, are you asleep?"

Rainer had the door closed before he fully registered another person in the cabin with him. Businessman sort, with a slightly weathered (or battered) face, fair suit, attaché case.

"Just sit. Don't talk. Malcolm: drive."

It would take a few moments for Rainer to process his own outrage, and Barney had to tell him to shut up three more times.

A few more moments, for Rainer to think about diving out of a moving vehicle. No good. Several more moments, to fret. To look out the window at anything except the gunman sitting before him.

Finally: "I presume I'm being kidnapped."

That was a laff riot. "I need one thing from you, Mister Rainer. I need the location of Carl Ledbetter. Can you provide that?" The SIG was trained unwaveringly on Rainer's solar plexus, since he probably didn't have a heart.

Rainer looked left, right, to the heavens. No help or guidance seemed imminent. Up close his face was even redder than the photograph, now going deeper crimson with barely suppressed fury. He blew out a breath like a snort. "Carl? That *loser*? Why, did he ass-rape you, too?" He seemed to rearrange his body to reassert his dominance, getting huffy. "And, Malcolm? You're fired."

To lend this man even a sense of his own superiority when confronted with lesser beings was a mistake, so Barney put a .357 round into the seat near Rainer's shoulder. The blast boxed their ears with concussion in the airtight seal of the limo cabin. Barney was used to the noise; most people were not. Malcolm flinched but kept his cool. *Sit, stay*. His hands jumped off the wheel but quickly reseated themselves. Rainer had contracted into a fetal ball, knees in his face, almost ready to evacuate his bladder all over his nice leather seats. Nobody outside the vehicle noticed the flash-pop of muzzle blast. Rich folks, probably, taking snapshots.

"Malcolm says you have a dinner date. Now you can be late as in tardy, or late as in deceased. Pick one. I don't want to kill you right now, but I will. Carl Ledbetter. Where?"

"You fucking asshole!" Rainer fumed. "Who are you?"

Barney leaned forward with the gun as if to fire again, feeling the neck strap cinch tight to make his aim rock steady. Rainer tried to astral-project and failed. "All right, all right, Jesus!" He was meekly reaching into his coat pocket.

"That hand comes out with anything on the end of it but a manicure, you're done," said Barney.

"Phone," said Rainer. "You can talk to him yourself. I don't want anything to do with whatever it is."

"Slide it," said Barney, not dumb enough to reach for it.

Carl Ledbetter had a New York City number.

"Can I have a drink, please?" said Rainer.

"No. Stay put. Malcolm, keep driving. Go around the park."

Barney punched the number. Something in his gut roiled. Carl answered on the third ring. Moment of dead air. Showtime.

"Hey, Carl. Sorry I didn't get back to you sooner."

Pause, for disbelief. There was no mistaking Barney's voice, no save and no waffle leeway for Carl.

It would take every ounce of fiber Carl possessed not to hang up and run. Barney knew Carl knew that, or was realizing it right this second. He had just enough free time to try sucking air. Maybe he would faint.

"Tell me where you are, Carl, or your pal Felix is going to die an extremely messy and disgusting death. No meeting place. No rendezvous. Where you are right now. You stay there until I get there. Answer now."

Imagine hearing the voice of a long-dead relative or

loved one, and think about how you would react. *Blasé* is not among the potential multiple choice answers.

Carl babbled. Corrected himself. Added superfluous detail. Said it all again. Once was enough. Barney hung up on him in mid-sentence

Barney kept watch on Malcolm. "Just keep doing what you're doing." There was a possibility that Malcolm might ram the limo into a parked car, dump himself free, and run for his life while his former boss ate a lot of bullets. Barney would have to bail and walk, blending into the pedestrians, losing the gun en route. Malcolm *might* have tried that; he certainly had the iron for it. But he had just been gracelessly sacked.

At Central Park West and 71st, Barney said, "Stop the car, Malcolm." He moved to disembark, attaché case first. "Felix? Listen to me: If you ever see me again, it'll be because you tried to call out the dogs or track me down, or tried to phone up some kind of retribution. You're not hurt, just scared. Don't let that make you do something rash."

"Why don't *you* tell me what the hell I'm supposed to do?"

"Go back to your life. Enjoy your dinner. Enjoy all the rest of your days, because they're a gift I'm giving you right now. Do not squander this gift. Try not to hold it against Malcolm. He's a good guy."

Barney stepped out. Rainer had more to say. "Hey!" Barney expected some parting threat, some *you-can't-get-away-with-this* horseshit. But Rainer said, "If you see Carl, do us all a favor and kill the sonofabitch, and I'll forget you ever existed."

Ever the dealmaker, that Felix.

°

As soon as he was clear of Felix Rainer, no harm no foul, Barney called Carl's cell again, this time with specific instructions. The danger of Felix Rainer burning up his own phone as he vented anger and tried to vector on Carl was too great. Carl would have to be run around town a bit, from Barney's secure cellphone.

Barney told Carl to go to Penn Station, buy a ticket for Elizabeth, New Jersey, board the train, and commute. Then Barney cabbed back to where his anonymous car was stashed, and caught up with a rattled-looking Carl while he was still in the ticket line. Carl proved too shaken to arm himself or attempt to set up a sting. Carl generally had other guys do that sort of work. Ex-friends, for example.

"Walk with me," said Barney. "Twitch funny and I'll blow your heart right out onto the pavement."

For a moment Carl feigned surprise at seeing his old friend, then thought better of it. Like Rainer, he avoided Barney's gaze, submissive, willing to be led, or at least impelled. His dislodged tooth had been replaced—badly, the substitute being slightly yellower than the rest of his dentition. Cheap cap. Overall, Carl appeared badly used by his most recent fiscal year.

"What do you want?" said Carl sullenly. He was in the bag and he knew it.

"Let's start with your wallet."

Carl started to say *you're kidding*, but no comedy waited in Barney's gaze. He mutely relinquished the same wallet Barney had seen in Mexico, containing the same picture of Erica, which was the only thing Barney appropriated. He handed the wallet back as though it was roadkill. Carl had exactly twenty-two bucks in cash.

"Yeah, take her," said Carl, still moping. "Keep her. I wish I'd never met that creature. *You* deal with her. You're welcome to her. I hope you're up to it."

Barney ignored the obvious bait.

Carl tried another tack: "How did you get to Felix?"

"Irrelevant. Tell me about Mexico."

"Oh, god, there was nothing I could do! I tried, but there was no way out—"

"You left me for dead. I didn't die."

"—and I'm so goddamned sorry, man, you know how it went, I couldn't help it—"

"Stop; I'm getting all misty over how much of a damn you gave for me. The money. Your little friends in the kidnapping business. Stay on track."

"That bastard Tannenhauser promised that—" Carl saw Barney's expression and clammed up. He clarified: "The guy in charge of the hostage hotel."

"Tannenhauser," said Barney. *El Chingon* had a name at last.

"Erica was banging him the whole time. But she outfoxed him and managed to scoot with most of the money—over a million-five."

"Wasn't Felix irritated about that?"

"*Felix?* Man, Felix didn't give a crap. All he did was ice me out."

There was no shortage in the world of greedy people looking for short cuts to financial success, as far as Felix Rainer was concerned. There was always fresh meat, or in Felix's parlance, "fungible commodities." If one deal went rancid, you divorced yourself from the particulars and concentrated on the next deal in the hopper.

Barney resisted the urge to grill Carl about the

pipeline, about how Felix Rainer could see some sort of obscure profit from this labyrinthine process, or how Carl and Erica were supposed to make out using other people's money. It didn't matter. It was like most scores: There was a prize, and everybody was screwing everybody else to get it. It did not need to be made legitimate or sensible via reverse-logic, it was a classic black-box scenario. Doesn't really matter what's in the box. What matters is whether you might get killed for it, and how you could better your odds.

"One last thing: the blond fellow you sent to kill me. He didn't make it."

Honest confusion drained further color from Carl's face. He had no idea what Barney was talking about. Score another point for Erica.

"Are you talking about a…a…hit man?"

"Yes, Carl. The kind of man you hire to do the sort of things you are too much of a coward to do. Like the way you lie to old friends so they'll stop a bullet you've earned—a warm body to throw to the wolves so you can skate and pretend you're innocent."

Carl's lips worked dryly against each other. He was taking his medicine like a punished child who thought the word *sorry* could set him free.

"If Erica is the heartless criminal mastermind you made her out to be, how did she get the money away from you?"

"We left Mexico on separate flights. When I landed I found out she'd flown to a different city."

"Why didn't Felix go after her?"

"What for? His deal was with me, period."

"Where is Erica now?"

"I wish I could tell you. I don't know. I really have

no idea, for almost a year, now." Carl mustered a bit of gall, enough to add, "But what about you? How did you—?"

"Doesn't matter," Barney interposed.

Barney had steered him between Eighth and Ninth, on 35th Street, walking west toward the Javits Convention Center.

"I'm telling you, you can shoot me, torture me, whatever, but I can't tell you what I don't know."

They stopped. Cabs soared by. It was dark now.

"I know this sounds stupid," said Carl, "but I'm glad you made it." Right about now, Carl would say anything or perform any abasement just to keep breathing. He tried to play the buddy-buddy card. "You know that little piece of the GPS you stashed in my coat? I didn't find out about it until they stopped me at the airport. I set off the damned alarm. That was pretty slick. I should have listened to you more…"

Barney put his hand on Carl's shoulder in a comradely gesture. This was supposed to be the part where all was forgiven in gruff camaraderie. "Okay, Carl, I believe you. But you shouldn't have left me twisting. Just shouldn't have."

Before Carl could respond, Barney jammed the SIG into his chest and fired two rounds completely through him. Before Carl could slump, Barney jammed the SIG under his jaw and blew the top of his head— and whatever else Carl was thinking—upward into the westerly breeze in a fine red spray.

The killing had begun.

Barney did not get a single drop on him. He was clean.

✳

Action is transient. Context takes the rest of forever.

You've really lost it now, Barney thought. *Let your anger boil over and get the better of you.*

Shooting Carl Ledbetter on a public street in the middle of New York City was almost a reflex action. It freighted no pang of guilt or remorse. It was what needed to be done. Barney could tell by the way Carl was losing his wits and trying to dissemble that he was attempting to buy talking time to forge fresh lies, to con him, to excuse what he had done by saying it was just business, not personal. That was how Carl's death had been—impersonal.

Strategically it was a matter of sheer gut sense. It was time. But Barney still felt played. He had done exactly what Felix Rainer had wanted, like a puppet or a robot. A hit man.

You've ignored gunshots, even though their sudden sound attracted your attention. Ninety-nine times out of a hundred, you dismissed or rationalized it: *That's not really gunfire. It's a backfire. It's construction noise.* It's always something else. That was how Barney could shoot a man three times and walk away. He was just another pedestrian who chose not to notice. Less than a block away, a gunshot made even less difference. Citizens ignored these sounds. They kept their noses down and minded their own damned business... although usually making sure to travel *away* from wherever the distressing sound originated. The same thing happened when someone screamed in the night. People shut their windows, turned their backs, cranked up the TV.

In seconds, Barney became just another person hurrying away from something potentially nasty, focused on doing the Manhattan shuffle, hands in pockets, eyes down. Had he lingered, he would have seen several other New Yorkers gingerly step around the fallen man on the sooty sidewalk. *He's a bum, a drunk, that's not really blood, that's not half his head gone; I'm just seeing things.*

Barney walked north along the Hudson, disassembling the SIG, dumping the parts and ammo. His gun hand had begun trickling threads of blood.

He flew back to Los Angeles that night, using a standby scheme that was a fringe benefit of Sirius' airline connections.

By the time Felix Rainer recovered his senses, he had nobody to look for and nobody to consult, since Carl was no longer talking.

Karlov asked, "How was the gun?"

"Perfect," Barney told him.

Armand asked, "How was the ammo?"

"Primo," Barney told him.

Sirius asked, "How was New York?"

"I can take the city for about ten days at a spell," Barney told him. "But longer than that and my skin begins to itch."

"How are your hands?" one of them asked.

"Well, I can still feed myself and wipe my own ass, which I count as progress."

"Find out what you needed?" another of them asked.

Felix Rainer had been willing to sacrifice Carl Ledbetter, and Carl had been eager to sacrifice Erica, if only she could be found. Dead end. It really did start to look as though she had outsmarted everyone, and Carl had never even met this person who was responsible for his heavy losses. Never seen her live, in the flesh. She was the best ghost of all, an unbeatable mystery. What was the next link in the string, when everybody was equally willing to eat their own soldiers?

Armand said, "You look spent, amigo."

"Yeah," said Barney. "I'm gonna sleep now, lapse into a coma I feel I've earned. I have to check in with Dr. Brandywine. Two days, say, to lock and load. Then you guys suit up, because we're going to Mexico."

The four fishing enthusiasts wearing aloha shirts and tinted sports sunglasses assembled in the bar at the Hotel del Rey to discuss their strategies for bagging swordfish and marlin once they received shipment of their fishing gear and caught a connecting flight to Mazatlan, after tonight's recreational stopover in Mexico City.

Their conversation was *extremely* boring.

The pallet holding their heavily insured custom fishing equipment was marked PRIORITY - CUSTOMS - EXPEDITE, and sailed through clearances with barely a nod of notice. As El Atrocidad had counseled, nobody smuggles stuff *into* Mexico…and that was not even considering the art of properly placed *baksheesh*, the bribe, a.k.a. *el soborno* or *la mordida*, literally "a little bite."

The next day, once they checked out of the Hotel del Rey, they simply vanished. Happens all the time in Mexico. It happened to a hundred thousand people a year in the United States. People got lost, got waylaid. Got murdered and never found. Went underground. Changed identities. Advantaged ironclad credit for other people who never existed in the first place. They ran from spouses, assumed disguises, ducked under Witness Protection, or just plain etherized without a trace. Out of nearly seven billion people on the entire planet, the percentage was microscopic, not even worth mentioning.

When Barney introduced his crew to the hidden wonders of La Pantera Roja, it took Armand nearly a full minute to stop laughing. He buttoned his mirth when Barney informed him that a special deal had been cut with the management of the sex motel—absolute privacy for a premium price. The desk man, an avaricious toad named Umberto Somethingorother, had winked knowingly. *Sí, comprendo totalmente.*

"You told him we're all *gay*?" Armand roared.

"Not in so many words, but it's not a first for him," said Barney. "Just tip big for his shitty microwave food and we'll be fine."

They swept the room for surveillance cameras or mikes and found none. There was a wall mount bored out behind a huge velvet painting of a naked Amazonian temptress (the frame hard-bolted to the beams, like everything else in the room), but nothing had been hooked up to it for years.

Each man set to the task of cleaning and checking equipment with a minimum of chitchat. They were no longer acting the part of visitors on fishing holiday and silently subsumed to their tasks with knowledge and competence—no rivalries, few jokes. The talk, the sizing up and slapjack of weapons, the speculations were for men between battles, not rubbing elbows with crunch time.

For the dirty and dangerous outing Barney had in mind, he had no wish to involve his local allies near the city, but he decided to risk a phone call to El Atrocidad in order to find the best and quickest way to procure a nondescript, used vehicle. As it turned out, the big wrestler was already involved. Past his pleasure and bonhomie at hearing Barney's voice and learning he was still among the living, Atrocidad shared the bad news:

"Amigo, you remember Flecha de Jalisco?"

"Of course," said Barney. The gravel-voiced *técnico* in whose debt he would always remain. "Cristobal. I hope nothing bad has happened."

"His son, Almirante, was taken by *los secuestradores* last week. They demand a ransom, or will start cutting off his fingers."

The news hit Barney like a body blow.

"There is something very interesting about these criminals," said Atrocidad. "They specified a money drop at the bridge on the Rio Satanas."

"I think I know where they might be keeping him," said Barney. He described the brown brick building where he had captured Carl Ledbetter. "It's in a bad part of the city, a freefire zone, like Neza."

He pictured El Atrocidad going crimson with fury. "Can you find it?!"

The implication was that an army of incognito luchadors stood ready to rush the walls in a beefy, un-stoppable wave.

"Give me a day, *camarado*. I promise I won't leave you out. But, and this is *muy importante*, how many days for the money?"

"*Dos dias mas.*"

"All right, two more days. Tell Flecha that if he speaks to the *secuestradores*, to tell them he has the

money, whatever amount it is. That he will make the
drop exactly as instructed."

"But he doesn't have the money yet."

"By tomorrow, amigo, they'll have bigger problems
than hurting Almirante—that's my promise, too."

"You are going to fight these *culos*? Not without me,
not without Flecha and Medico Odio and—"

"*Calmasé*," said Barney. "You're not going to be left
out."

El Atrocidad struggled with this for a moment, then
cleared his throat and said, "Your word, that is enough."

"My word. On *mi vida*. You keep your cellphone by
you at all times."

A modification to Barney's plan had presented itself,
and it solved a lot of problems. He had no desire to
put these good men in harm's way, but the resolution
struck him with such clarity that it seemed perfectly,
immediately, obviously important.

They were able to purchase outright a blue paneled
van with a cracked windshield and most of the tread
still on the tires, from a nephew of El Atrocidad's who
had managed to keep himself blissfully uninvolved
with killers or kidnappers. The van stayed nicely low-
profile in the Pantera Roja's conveniently conceived
security carport.

It fell to Barney to explain to his companions that
they now had a complication…and a clock.

They switched their tourist duds for job clothes
—loose, but not enough to snag; dark, but not so
dark as to prevent ID by a friendly. Under their
garments, Armand's special body armor covered them
in two pieces from mid-thigh to upper arm, about
T-shirt length. Without the side zippers, donning them

would have been like trying to squeegee into wet rubber.

Everybody paused to marvel at the bullet scars on Barney's torso, which Barney endured with something like resigned tolerance. He drew the line at letting Karlov measure them.

"I didn't know you wore jewelry," said Armand, pointing at the polished agate nestled tight to Barney's collarbone by a leather thong.

"Not jewelry," returned Barney, his hand moving reflexively to touch the stone Mano had given him.

Karlov tossed Barney a pair of gloves—Blackwater Armor Skins tacticals with Kevlar, re-sewn to Barney's hand dimensions and modified to keep his trigger fingers free.

"Just in case you start leaking again," Karlov said.

They all wore ATAC Storm SWAT boots, night-shade cargo pants and zippered "511"-style response jackets. Each was kitted out with a fixed-blade knife and MagLite in addition to their chosen weaponry. The guns had been cleaned and checked, then checked again, then field stripped and checked, before being re-checked. Four to five mags maximum for the semi-autos—an overload of weight made it impossible to sustain an aggressive operational tempo, by encumbering maneuverability and causing fatigue.

Sirius had suggested handcuffs in case they needed to incapacitate anyone in transit; these were snug in scabbards and would bounce no light. Sirius was also the man who carefully polished each cartridge and loaded each mag wearing surgical gloves to prevent ejected brass from providing fingerprints.

Any item not mission-essential was dumped. You

don't carry spare change into a hot zone because the jingle might give you away. Ditto keys and what the pros called "mental comfort items." They had Nomex watch caps which could be pulled down into ski-masks if needed.

Barney had driven the route in his stolen BMW more than a year ago, but nothing had changed. They hit the building at two in the morning…

…not that the atmosphere of deadly carnival was any different at that time of day in this hellhole, which defied the lockstep concept of business hours.

"That's where Carl went in," Barney said, indicating the iron speakeasy door recessed into a dark entryway.

"How about the roof?" said Sirius.

"No idea."

"Give me the case."

Armand handed over a Halliburton knock-off they had doctored back at the Pantera Roja—stacks of trimmed rag paper with bona fide $100 bands, and a genuine bill on top of each. Barney thumb-checked his SIG .40, his batter-up gun, to ensure chambered brass.

They scattered from the van so as not to cross the street in a group. There was a small traffic island to get past, not to mention assorted panhandlers, hucksters and prostitutes eager to triangulate on a non-Hispanic face. Barney was first in, all business as he rapped on the metal-sheeted door.

A glowering monster peeked out with cloudy, mud-colored lizard eyes. Barney said nothing and exhibited the case.

"*Mostramé*," said a clotted voice.

Barney displayed the money in the case, careful not to expose it to street view. *"¡Apúrate!"* he said. *Hurry up*.

Five deadbolts threw back and a squeaky latch was undogged.

At the first crack of dim light from within, several things happened simultaneously. Barney hit the door full force, wedging the briefcase into the crack and prying a foot of open space. Karlov and Armand were already behind him, guns up. Sirius barreled through last, making Barney's impact with the door and his own into one sustained breach. The bandana-wearing creep inside the door was propelled against the far wall in a narrow corridor, and was already bringing a nasty-looking .45 revolver into play. Sirius was quicker with his own .45, a Para-Ordnance Tac-Five LDA from which Karlov had removed the grip safety. He had two of them. Sirius dealt the slide to the guy's skull, a left-right combo that rocked him like a bobble-head doll and rolled his eyeballs up into nighty-night.

They were bulling right into a range instructor's nightmare: Unknown space in hallways always consti-tuted a kill zone, and this one went in two directions, making a linear entry per the designates of close-quarter combat impossible. The goal is always to "col-lapse" the space—that is, mass your fire and visually pick up threats as fast as possible.

Barney had gone low to cover right while Armand slipped behind Sirius to cover left. Karlov backed through last, covering their backsides, stepping over the unconscious mug on the floor, as both ends of the hallway began to fill with armed men shouting alarm.

This was what Barney's team had come for. Hitting

a paper target is one thing. Winning a combat competition on a freestyle range against plywood jump-up assailants is another. Stalking and shooting a game animal, same-same. Hitting a moving target in gunfire and chaos, a target that is shooting back at you, is quite a different thing altogether, a biochemical state of mind/body fusion that cannot be simulated, at least not in the ways that count.

Each man was fit enough to recover solid shooting positions multiple times during an engagement, therefore healthy enough to affect quicker healing if hit. You don't rely on the weapon to solve all your problems; you need strength, stamina, endurance, speed and the ability to "see before shooting"—that is, process threat information faster than your opponent—as well as the golden rule of servicing a bad guy: *Shoot until they drop*. This was the difference between live-fire training and real life; between a shooting and a gunfight. A shooting is unidirectional. A gunfight happens when the thing you are shooting at has the ability to shoot back.

A slug from a pocket pistol zinged off the wall near Sirius' head as Karlov slammed and latched the door. Barney already had the shooter so framed he did not need his sights, put two in his chest from the SIG, and watched the man's flung pistol bounce off the ceiling as his buddies hared back to cover. Armand did not wait to be shot at, and emptied the cylinder of his behemoth Ruger at the far end of his zone in a circular pattern that convinced a lot of people to be somewhere else. Through the gunsmoke Barney picked out an arm hit, a leg hit, and another uncertain—three down from the destructive power of a full-charge .44

Magnum cartridge meant three that would not come
back into gunplay.

They moved as a group toward the Barney side of
the hall with hard practical cover in all directions.
Armand ejected his spent brass and nearly fumbled
his speedloader. His hands were shaking, not with fear
or incompetence, but excitement.

The initial response group, ragged and disorganized,
was mostly retreating across a large interior atrium,
just the sort of open space Barney had predicted the
building would have. Sporadic gunfire came back at
them, but it was unaimed, over-the-shoulder stuff.
Barney popped one guy's hogleg right out of his hand,
then looked up to witness the spectacle of Karlov,
arms extended, firing in two directions at once with his
twin nine-millimeters—back the way they came and
ahead of them, and scoring crippling hits both ways. A
bouncing piece of hot brass jabbed Barney's cheek.

Then somebody opened up on them from the second floor with more serious artillery, a full-sized Uzi
carbine from the sound and delivery. Apparently the
shooter did not care that Uzis tend to pull up and to
the right on full-auto fire, and a double tap from Sirius'
.45 put the man away before he could correct his aim.

Karlov took two more stragglers from a kneeling
position as Sirius fired over his head. Barney indicated
a stairway to the second floor, and Sirius moved on it,
Armand second. Incoming fire was light and undisci-
plined. Somehow Barney had expected these guys to
be better shots, but then he remembered how they
had handled machine guns at the bridge.

At the second-floor landing a pair of dazed women
screamed and dropped flat, probably unintentionally,

but it was the best cover they could have hoped for. A gunless guy with matted hair and no shoes did a spin-around in the hall, trying to figure out which way to run.

People were screaming and pell-melling to get out of the way, and very few of them had guns.

Barney kicked in the nearest door—no lock. He was afforded excellent cover by his men on the stairs and landing as he proceeded down a row of doors, coming through each one gun-first and then backing off without firing.

A hotshot young gunslinger with something to prove tried to nail Karlov on the stairs, and Karlov took some splinters in the face from the balustrade as bullets bit into the lumber. Sirius sent him packing with hazing fire that destroyed all the masonry around the man's head. Sirius, too, had already sensed something was awry.

Barney double-timed it back to the group. "It's an abort!" he shouted. "Everybody bail!"

They encountered only three more men with guns as they escaped through the rear of the building.

One man saw them coming, dropped his peashooter, and ran.

One man managed to hit Armand in the shoulder, and Sirius kneecapped him from a distance of twenty yards, firing one-handed—five shots for one hit.

The third man brought a shotgun to bear, a double-barreled howitzer loaded with 12-gauge buck, and they all felt the pellets. Then Armand, Barney and Karlov raised and fired as one, and separated the guy from his piece.

It had all seemed far too easy.

Back in the van they were panting, sweat-drenched and pawing at their collateral damage. Finally, Sirius said, "Okay—what the hell just happened?"

"Sorry, guys," Barney said. "Wrong building." His hands were bloody in more ways than one.

They all just looked at him, waiting for a punchline.

Barney told them what he had seen when he kicked in the first second-floor door, the door that, not to put too fine a point on it, had no lock. Inside were candles sputtering in wine bottles and an assortment of junkies sprawled like sniper victims, barely able to register the entrance of a man with a gun. They flopped about on dirty mattresses or stared at infinity points in space. Next room, same deal—freebasing crackheads and a *mamacita* on the nod who was trying to coax milk out of one flaccid tit to feed an infant who was either comatose or dying.

Wrong building. These were all victims of a different kind of kidnapping, with none of the administrative smell that would have told Barney he was in the right place. It featured the correct ratio of coke-addled meatheads with guns for a drug den, with the primary shooters being security and management. They were also the first to run, clearing out and marooning their ex-customers to find their own way.

Carl Ledbetter and Mister *El Chingon* Tannenhauser must have used this place as a meeting point, meaning the real hostage hotel could be anywhere within a radius of miles. The courtyard fit, but dozens of structures in this neck of the woods had them.

Wrong building.

Worse, Barney's bad guess had just dropped Flecha

de Jalisco's son Almirante into the hot pot with the real kidnappers. The phone call confirming the money Flecha had *not* raised had already been made, on El Atrocidad's advice, on Barney's word.

The impact bruise on Armand's shoulder was a blue-black starburst that grated his bones, but the liquid body armor had worked like a magic shield in a fairy tale. Karlov's facial wounds were superficial.

"Yeah," Sirius said when they were back at the Pantera Roja, "Except that we just shot seventeen or eighteen of the wrong guys."

"No," said Karlov, dipping witch hazel and antiseptic cream. "When you said you were in, that meant you were in even for this."

"I didn't shoot at anyone who didn't shoot at me first, and that was the deal," said Armand, nursing his shoulder.

"It's on me," said Barney. "I was sure that was the place. I was dead wrong. And now they're going to slice off Almirante's fingers one by one unless we find out where they really are."

"Owww, damned shotgun got me right in the *neck*," Armand complained when he saw the pellet track an inch from his carotid artery. They all had dimpled bruises from the shot, as though a finger had been dipped in ink and pressed to the skin. They were painful but the body armor had done its task and rendered them down from lethal.

Barney sight-profiled all of them and the chatter dropped to nil. The question before them was clear: *We have weathered an accident and come out whole. It gets worse. Anybody wants to bail, raise a hand.* The moment held for a few beats, then dissipated as though it never existed. Nobody left. Each man took turns at the mirror checking their wear and tear.

"So what do we do?" said Sirius, who found three dark dots delineating his waist on the left.

"We take the ransom drop. It's a bluff, and we're stuck with it, so let's play it all the way. The difference is, now we have to snag one of the bad guys and not waste any time sweating him." He cracked a crooked half-smile and stared at the floor. "I've done it before."

Bulling in full-strength and unidirectionally was not the way to approach the Rio Satanas bridge drop. They had one day left on the ransom clock and Barney took them to the target twelve hours ahead of schedule, for best placement based on what he remembered from the first ransom delivery.

"The minute there's gunfire, the *secuestradores* will know the deal has curdled," said Barney. "It'll take about two seconds for somebody to spread the news on a cellphone, and thanks to me, Almirante will probably lose a finger before they double their demands, but better a finger than a life."

"No need to keep blaming yourself," said Karlov. His face was dotted with little circular Band-Aids he had smeared to neutral with camo paint.

But Barney felt the bite of irony; it had him captured like a narcotic. His negligence would cause Almirante to lose fingers. He did his best to refocus his embarrassment into aggression, then froze fast in wonder at the fact he was concerned at all. Dormant feelings had roused deep inside him. He was not the reincarnation of the Old Assassin after all, or if he was, the sage old killer had been resurrected with a vulnerability, a soft spot. Emotion, however primal, had entered his target's sight picture, and at that, Barney should have quit and withdrawn. You could not permit an objective to become polluted. His gratitude to the people who had saved his life had just been shoved into hot focus by the fact he was no longer acting solely on behalf of his vendetta, but to save the skin of one of their own.

The best course was to hop-to and not fuck it up, this time. He could psychoanalyze himself later, because right now there was brutal work to do.

Barney indicated the primary shooter slots, the directions from which the late Jesús and his runner buddies had hared forth to collect the cash, and the most likely strategic positions for cover and observation. Tannenhauser, the Mexican with the unlikely name and principal architect of the art of abduction, had been nearby when Carl and Barney had showed up the first time. Not only had he watched, probably through binoculars (which could put him a thousand yards away, or better), but he had gloated to Carl over the hostage cellphone in such a way as to indicate he was indeed seeing the whole exchange live.

But the boss would probably not attend tonight. In business, one learns from experience.

There was no way *not* to tell El Atrocidad.

"I and three of my friends will be waiting," Barney said into the phone. "We don't want to have to deal with friendly fire. Our objective is to capture one of the pickup men. Repeat, *capture*—not kill."

"So you cannot locate the hotel of the *rehéns*?"

"No, my information was unreliable. I know Almirante is at risk, but we must take that risk." Barney could not quite bring himself to admit out loud that he had screwed the pooch once already.

"You risk not only yourself, but your men," returned Atrocidad gruffly. "For one of ours. We shall not bring *las armas* if you tell me that you will."

"Consider your ass covered, big man."

If anything, the meltdown district where the oddly fanciful bridge was located smelled even worse than Barney remembered. No memory puckers the pores like decomposing sewage and toxic spill. Karlov wore his shooting glasses with flip-down tinted lenses—he was a bit nearsighted—and within moments they all had mufflered themselves in bandanas in a futile attempt to filter the stench. You wanted to cover as much of your skin as possible in a place like this; even taking a sip of bottled water seemed hazardous, because the water made the briefest contact with the air before it got inside you. Nothing had any color here, beyond iron-gray and mud-brown. Nothing grew on the eroded banks of the river where La Llorona was said to call out in the night, at the full moon.

As the sun descended, the evil, poisoned ground gave up more odor in thick waves of released heat. The men were already sweltering in their gear, but to inhale a double lungful of this aroma was to induce vomiting.

Barney unsheathed one of the Benelli shotguns. He was positioned so as to neutralize the bridge shooter who had surprised him the first time. Different cast, same movie, only now Barney was the screen, looking at the audience. Two hours before the appointed meet, two full-size, flat-black SUVs with nonreflective rims showed up to disgorge about fifteen men. Barney's team was secreted around the perimeter, concealed beneath reeking garbage and industrial litter, their faces eliminated by camouflage paint.

They all went hot on their conferenced cellphones, another tweak of Karlov's.

"I can see the vehicles," came Armand's voice in a crackle. He was invisible somewhere off to Barney's left. "They pulled back about forty yards, by the oil pumpers, whatever you call those things that look like dunk-birds. Two and two."

Correction: *nineteen* men, all armed.

"Armand, take the cars," said Barney.

"Copy, take cars and men. Done."

"I've got five on my side of the river," said Karlov. "Flanking out from the cars. They look to be cover fire or surprise backup. I can take these five but I've got to move closer for the rest."

A phalanx of the men crossed the bridge and scattered, leaving a solitary shooter up top. No way there had been this many guys when Carl and Barney had first visited. Tannenhauser's idea of security had gone practically American—*more* equals *better*.

"I've got men heading under the bridge," said Sirius, slightly further back in a crow's nest position with the Nitefinder binoculars.

"Can you get them all?" said Barney.

"You might have to pick up some spare change on your way over. Karlov, you've got two more moving up on your six o'clock." Not good. Karlov's hide now had shooters on both sides of it.

"Copy," said Karlov. "Betcha a beer I can take seven before you take five."

Sirius replied, "Meet me after. These are some scruffy-looking dudes indeed." As an afterthought he added, "Packing autos; watch out for spray."

"Complaints, complaints," Karlov chimed in through a brief jolt of static. "Grow up. This is fewer than five each, and I have what you call the handicap."

Armand's voice came back: "I can take the bridge shooters from behind."

"Negative," said Barney. "Take the vehicles. Make sure they don't go anywhere."

"Copy."

"Take them on my shot," said Barney.

The sun ebbed and the shadows lengthened. It was getting crowded out here, thought Barney. The hidden watchers were themselves being watched by his team, better concealed.

At the appointed time , when the fetid atmosphere was bristling with anticipation, Barney saw El Atrocidad's golden chariot slowly negotiate its way over roads that were little better than sodden goatpaths. It stopped the same distance from the bridge that Barney had stopped Carl's limo, in another time.

Flecha debarked from the passenger side—Barney recognized the tank-shaped man immediately—which meant El Atrocidad was in the driver slot. The car was roughly between Sirius to the south, and Karlov to the north on the far side of the river.

He saw Flecha raise a cellphone to his ear.

Barney dog-crawled from his hide. He did not need nightvision, though he was aware the enemy probably had it.

Flecha repeated his instructions, his low purr of a voice audible, though not intelligible.

With the semi-auto Benelli in a low-ready dedicated carry, Barney did a double roll to bring him in
line with the pathway on the bridge and fired twice
from a distance of fifteen running yards. The shooter
on the bridge screamed and fell over, pretty much a
sieve from the knees up.

Gunfire perforated the night, muzzle flashes everywhere as the dumping ground transmogrified into a
battlefield.

Sirius took the bridge runners, one-two-three, as
they broke cover and started firing machine guns at
Atrocidad's car.

Karlov took the backup men, having correctly estimated the direction each of them would move once
gunshots galvanized them. He poked up from his comfy
foxhole and revolved like a gun turret, delivering both
hi-cap mags—a blistering salvo of forty-four rounds—
in under ten seconds, shooting both of his nines at
once. Then he dropped out of sight like a jack in the
box with second thoughts. His seven men were all
down, dead or howling.

Barney ran across the bridge, eating up the real
estate between him and the two SUVs, one of which
was already moving. Two rounds from Armand's
Benelli caused the rear tires to shred apart and the
chunky car sat down hard, ass-skidding into a crooked
pyramid of rusty 40-gallon drums. Barney put his final
four rounds through the windshield, which imploded
in a sparkling black hailstorm of safety glass. Armand
had command of the other car already.

Barney dropped the shotgun and cross-drew his
.40, approaching the vehicles in a heel-and-toe step,
careful not to cross one leg in front of the other and
get tangled in his own limbs.

Sirius answered incoming auto weapons fire with his own shotgun. Then Barney heard the distinct cannonade of Sirius' .44 clipping stragglers.

Start to finish, something like twenty seconds.

Gunsmoke spiced the toxic wind.

"Hey, amigo!" It was Atrocidad's voice, coming from the car. "You there? I have a present for you!" The big wrestler's guttural signature laugh echoed in the sudden silence.

Barney hustled over while his team checked the dead and the dying, to make sure no opponent could zombie up and start shooting again.

"Heeeeeyyyyyy!" Atrocidad's grin was so wide that Barney was afraid it would split his face and make the top of his head fall off. He was holding a ransom runner by the scruff and randomly punching him whenever he twitched. The smaller man's feet were off the ground.

"Look at you!" Atrocidad bellowed. "You're up, you're walking, you're fighting, life is good!" He punched his captive again. "You'll pay for my paintjob, *pinche cabron*." Then he dropped his insensate prisoner like a mail sack and wrapped Barney up in a bear hug.

Flecha de Jalisco was smiling big as well, even though he had one massive hand clamped over his bicep, which was leaking blood through his suit. He gave Barney a thumbs-up. No big deal.

"It's good to see you," said Barney. "But we're going to have to hold off on the celebration and reunion for a bit."

"We know," said Atrocidad. "But meanwhile, check this *puto*."

El Atrocidad dragged his charge in front of the Cadillac's headlamps.

Barney's mouth belayed into a stall of disbelief. Even past the blackening eyes and ruptured nose, he could still recognize the guy Atrocidad had stopped on the run.

"Well, I'll be goddamned and completely gone to hell if it's not my old pal Condorito." The skittish monkey-man from the hostage hotel, the one who had participated in Barney's beatings after Sucio and the others had softened him up. Barney grabbed a fistful of his rank hair and got in his face. "This is a rare honor. It's not every day I get to watch somebody's life turn to shit right before their eyes, and today, old buddy, that somebody is you." He held the dazed man's head in his hands, resisting the urge to smash it to pulp with his SIG.

Armand came humping up. "Karlov's hit. We have to get the hell outta here, pronto."

A 9-millimeter slug from an HK MP5 had bored into Karlov's forearm below the elbow, and boy, was he piqued.

"Damn stupid dumb luck," he griped. Lacking a field dressing, he applied pressure to the entry and exit wounds by plugging his thumb and middle fingers into the holes and grimacing a lot. Karlov had stamina, no doubts there.

A brief debate ensued over whether Atrocidad should take him to the hospital along with Flecha, whose pistol wound would be easier to explain. Karlov vigorously protested, saying he needed to get back to his toolkit, and a first aid box they had back at the motel. Too many questions and not enough time. He needed to concentrate on processing the trauma.

"Let me stay," said El Atrocidad after he had delivered Flecha to a *clínica* he knew close to Arena Coliseo. "You need little *puto* to tell you where *los secuestradores* are hiding; I can make him sing opera."

"It has to be fast," said Barney. "They'll be chopping off Almirante's fingers any minute now."

"*Sí, claro.* But a man can lose many fingers before he is dead." The wrestler opened his arms in brotherly entreaty. Barney himself was proof of what he said.

They wrung out Condorito in the motel room while Karlov treated his own gunshot wound. It was a toss-up as to which spectacle was bloodier.

Armand flinched when he saw Karlov ream out his arm with a sterilized barrel-cleaning brush. He poked it in one side and pulled it through the other while biting on a rolled-up washcloth, making a horrific noise like a prehistoric animal going down in a tar pit. Armand flinched again when he saw Karlov douse the tunnel with peroxide. The table flooded with pink fizzing foam dotted with tiny splashes of Karlov's sweat, dripping freely from his brows and chin. He packed the wound with antibiotic gel and wrapped it in gauze.

"If you'll pardon me now," Karlov said, "I am going to go vomit, and then lie down. Do not even think of telling me I am out of the op, because I am not."

"You can't do gunfire," Barney said, looking up from where he was dealing with Condorito on the far side of the room.

"I've got ten years on you, young man, so I outrank you. I just took down seven men firing two-handed. So don't tell me what I can and cannot do." Karlov shuffled off toward the bathroom, woozy from shock. He had a bit of trouble tacking on the doorway.

Barney returned his attention to Condorito, holding up the Smith & Wesson .22 revolver Karlov had given him. "Real simple. I shoot this through your foot, like so."

Barney placed the eight-inch barrel on top of Condorito's sneakered foot, beneath which El Atrocidad had lodged a phone book. The bang of the .22 was similar to the snap of a big mousetrap. They could shoot this piece in here all day and nobody would notice or care.

Condorito contracted in abrupt, undeniable pain. He could not kick or flail much; his extremities were all duct-taped to a tubular metal chair which Atrocidad held down in order to keep it from falling over as the smaller man juddered.

"Then," said Barney, "we remove this." He pulled a wadded towel from where it was crammed into Condorito's mouth. Condorito blubbered a string of insults and admonitions. "Then," Barney continued, "you tell us where the hostage hotel is, *comprendes*?"

Condorito offered several observations on the nature of pain, on Barney's sexual proclivities, and possible heritage.

Barney shot him in the other foot. *Bang*. Flush, rinse, repeat.

"Your knees are next. Then your hands. Then your elbows. Then I've got two shots left in this cylinder I haven't decided what to do with yet. You tell us where it is, because you're going to *show* us where it is, no matter how many holes I put in you."

There was a loud thump against the wall from the next room. Everybody held in position and caught their breath, except for Condorito. There was a pain demon trapped inside his skin, and it wanted out.

The men looked to each other. Another thump. No, a series of thumps, rhythmic. Then a muffled cry: *"¡Ayyy! ¡Ayyy! ¡Papi! ¡Mijo! ¡Ayy! ¡Ayy!"*

Somebody was ramming their dream date against the headboard in the adjacent room with slightly more abandon than you would expect from a comfortably married couple, which is to say a couple married to each other. La Pantera Roja did, after all, have many other paying customers.

"¡Ayy! ¡Alocate y haste mia! ¡Chupame la cola! ¡Ayy! ¡Ayy!"

El Atrocidad lit up the room with his grin as the others tried to match it.

Barney rolled his eyes and turned back to Condorito, gun in hand. "Nobody's going to hear the gun, not in this place, and for sure nobody's going to hear *you* squawking."

Not a particularly brave man when it came to saving his life, Condorito spilled everything he could think of. Area, street, security, size of opposing force. Layout. Anything that would keep him from getting married to another tiny wasp-like bullet. El Atrocidad nodded at Barney through some of it. Barney made Condorito repeat everything several times, faster and faster, so no a la carte lies could slip through. By the time he was finished, Condorito's palate was very familiar with the taste of the gun barrel.

"All right," said Barney. "Tape him up and get him into the van." The rest of their gear had been loaded by Armand and Sirius. "Don't forget the grenades this time."

Sirius winced. "Hey, I was all excited and shit, okay? Let it go." In his rush to first blood at the crack den he had forgotten the grenade bag; fortunately they hadn't needed it.

There was a more important reason for clearing out of the Pantera Roja: Once the kidnappers twigged to the massacre at the bridge, one of them might be smart enough to remember that the Pantera Roja was where they had re-acquired Jesús, and come calling with maximum warpower. It was safer to consider this base blown. Whatever came in the aftermath—food, showers, rest—would come at some other place, utterly unpredictable and totally anonymous.

"Amigo," said Atrocidad. "Pardon me for saying so, but—"

Barney whirled on him. "What?" This man was going to tell him what he was doing was sadistic and unfair, despite helping him do it. This man was going to lecture him on the differences between right and wrong, good and evil, and what was righteous and what was low.

El Atrocidad spoke measuredly, to insure he was not misunderstood. "I was just going to say, amigo, that you...ehh, stink. Smell really bad, you know?"

Barney had mopped off his camo but his eyes were still raccooned and black sweat tracks grooved his face. They all smelled like the septic tank of an abortion clinic at high tide.

"We haven't got time for a group shower," Barney said, collecting his refreshed clips from Armand. The motel room was thick with a humid inversion layer of butchershop blood and locker room secretions.

"That's what we do," said Sirius, holstering his Magnum. "We all stink together, baby."

Karlov rose from his cot to prove he was far from out of the game. "Or we most assuredly shall stink separately."

They had time for one swig from one beer Sirius had left in the fridge. They passed it around and it came to Barney last. He drained it, taking a unique pleasure in seeing Condorito eye the bottle as though it was the closest the little man would ever get to his version of Heaven.

El Atrocidad did his damnedest to tag along but Barney prohibited it. His mission was to assemble a group of Flecha's friends, luchadors all, and await a cue via cellphone. Barney stressed this. It was important to have the wrestlers involved, particularly since Flecha de Jalisco had himself been wounded in battle over his own son, but Barney convinced Atrocidad that it was even more important to wait for the cue. Timing was paramount, and if a ring superstar could not acknowledge that, he or she had no business waxing mythic.

Condorito, his gunshot feet padded in rags wrapped outside his sneakers, proved to be an adroit navigator once the right stimulus was applied. He even suggested shortcuts and alternate routes to avoid the worst of the traffic. From Barney's dim memory of roadbumps, halts and sudden turns taken while he was hooded and blind, they seemed to be on the right track. If they deviated due to trickery, he would smell it and gift Condorito with another bullet.

Karlov was in the back of the van drawing and holstering, trying to coax his injured arm up to specs. He had adopted one of the neck slings he had designed for Barney's aim and stayed busy adjusting it.

Armand was riding shotgun, and Sirius was next back, propping Condorito up between the seats to plot the course.

The Iztapalapa district west of Mexico City is a working class barrio ringed with shantytowns competing with monolithic, cinderblock industry, a fast lane in the superhighway of *narcotrafico* and crime, double-stuffed to bursting with overpopulation and violence-by-the-minute. Razed to the ground in the 16th Century by Hernan Cortez in a genocidal war against the Aztecs memorialized as the Sad Night, Iztapalapa was also the locale of Mexico's first school shooting spree by a student, in 2001. It is not found on the usual checklists of things to see and do in Mexico, yet paradoxically it becomes the locus for hundreds of thousands of visitors on Good Friday, when the populace goes mad reliving Golgotha—a reenactment of the Passion that has been going on since the 1830s, when the area was decimated by cholera. Fake Christs lug crosses; others tart up in a kind of Busby Berkley approximation of Roman centurions, and amid religious chants and simulated flagellation the crucifixion is dramatized on a southern hill that later turned out to be a lost pre-Columbian pyramid covered in dirt, with squatters encamped at its base.

Good Friday was months distant, though, and today Iztapalapa was just another urban war zone into which Condorito, wounded emissary, led warriors.

The building he called the *palacio* was a half-block-sized brick rectangle with—as Barney had correctly guessed a year earlier—a large interior courtyard accessed through armored doors. It was an old factory fortressed up similarly to the crackhouse they had invaded: bars, metal plating, no window entry, razorwire ringing the roof. The north wall was a gigantic, faded beer advertisement that was decades old and buried in graffiti.

They circled the building for a look-see, and half the circumference was on dirt roads with no names.

"That's where they go in," said Condorito, pointing to a gated archway in the south wall. It was well back from the street inside its own stone tunnel.

"Can we drive through that gate?" said Barney.

Condorito mulled this over. "You hit it at about forty, you probably knock it down, *sí*, but then a lot of guys be shooting at you."

"Sirius, how're those smoke grenades?"

"They'll do the job, like I said. But what I didn't get to say is that they're LZ markers."

Karlov said, "What is he talking about?"

"It's *colored* smoke," said Barney.

Armand lifted one out of the pouch and examined it. "Look, we've got flavors: red, orange, green, violet, blue, yellow."

"They're fine," protested Sirius. "Five vents, 50- to 90-second discharge, one-point-five second fuse."

"But they're in *colors*," Barney said with a slightly pained expression.

"Oh, climb outta my butt," Sirius said, his dander riled. "Look, we can even launch these out of the shotguns. See? Adapter. Click, bang, just like a TL-1."

"Okay, all right, as long as we've got coverage."

"In color," Armand said, refusing to turn loose of the joke.

"Well, this oughta be festive," said Barney. He turned to Condorito, who looked strung-out, but maintaining. "You positive *this* van can crash through *that* gate?"

"Yesss," he said, drawing the consonant out, which meant pretty sure. "It swings open." He demonstrated with his hands.

"*Bueno*," said Barney, "Because you're going to drive."

Picture the gate to the Palacio as the crossbar of the letter H, with the entry through the lower half. Inside that staple-shape a surveillance camera monitored the tunnel, which was arched, almost Moorish, from a tamper-proof mount high on the left. Dark inside. There was no security door cut into the gate; it was not designed to admit pedestrians. This was for deliveries.

Outside on the street, two men walked past the tunnel entryway, the bottom of the H. One paused, apparently to light a cigarette. The other continued walking.

When Sirius and Armand had bracketed the tunnel they each tossed in smoke. Red and yellow clouds combined to form a bilious orange, rather akin to a fire without the light or heat. It clogged the tunnel in five seconds. Sirius folded himself into the artificial fog bearing a shotgun adapted to fire the smoke cartridges. His station was upper left corner, below the now-blind camera, the elbow of the bottom of the H. Armand took right corner. Karlov was on standby outside. Under his coat he wore his fabulous four-gun holster rig.

Direct approach was impossible, due to the road jog and a dirt-surfaced side road that cut through the opposing block. The tunnel was meant to be turned into, not accessed head-on. The panel van lurched over the side-road, making about forty-five before it had to grab a sharp right and sail into the tunnel, like a trick-angle shot in billiards.

Taped into the driver's seat was Condorito, looking mildly insane, Barney's gun barrel nestled in his occipital ditch. To external view Condorito was just another lunatic Mexican driver hopped up on goofballs and playing the road as a video game. The van went briefly airborne after clearing a rut, and two wheels left the ground on the turn. They were hammering a solid half-buck when they split the smoke in the tunnel and struck the gate.

The stanchions securing the gate ripped out of concrete and eviscerated the van's transmission on the way through. Iron trespass teeth gutted the tires and the van nosed down sharply, grinding through on rims. The left arm of the gate flew free of its hinges and landed in the courtyard, sliding, striking sparks. The right arm banged back to fan the billow of smoke disgorging from the tunnel. The van fishtailed to a stop and sat there steaming, quickly enveloped by the smoke.

Inside the courtyard, men were yelling.

Sirius had stepped aside to let the van juggernaut past about a foot away from him. When his side of the gate vanished with a metallic clang he eeled around the corner, hugged the wall, and began to peg smokers around the perimeter. Karlov came through right behind him, quick-drawing his .40 with his good hand and potting two rounds through the chest of a sentry who was just regaining his senses enough to raise a weapon at Sirius.

On Armand's side, the swinging gate had center-punched another guard, who was just getting to hands and knees and groping around for his Uzi on the ground. Armand's Magnum blasted the guy into a surfer flip and he went down and stayed still.

Barney kicked out through the rear of the van as men on the second floor of the atrium opened up, full auto, on the intruder vehicle. Condorito died an inglorious death at the hands of his co-workers, shredded by bullets that vaporized the windshield, destroyed the cabin and made both him and the upholstery into floating chaff. What several hundred incoming bullets will do to an automobile—not mention the hapless bastard inside—is a minor miracle of horror.

An alarm klaxon began to bark, echoing in the courtyard, which was now fogged in with orange, then laced with green and blue as Sirius placed his smokers in what he called a "Dr. Pepper spread"—ten, two, and four o'clock.

The enemy, surprised and lacking visual targets, concentrated on the van. Barney's team had planned how to move, and did not necessarily need to see.

Barney knew this place. His ears knew it. His memory confirmed it. The graveled pavement beneath his feet was a sense picture. He had been muscled along this very surface with his head bagged. There would come a door, a narrow hallway, an elevator. The secured rooms that served as cells. Tannenhauser's office, brain central for the kidnapping ring. Barney remembered the toy soldiers grouped on one corner of Tannenhauser's computer desk. He and his men were the soldiers now, coming home.

Even with the best of intel, it had been impossible to plan textbook moves such as link-up points, limits of advance, areas of responsibility or fields of fire. Knowing they had to wing it, Barney's team stayed tight if for no other reason than to avoid shooting each other in the smokescreen.

Karlov tapped Armand on the arm and together they got a sight picture on Sirius. They married up and proceeded leftward, blasting the occasional running gunner back into the smoke. They found the east wall.

A door opened and two gunners came ready to fight. They looked up into a fusillade of bullets that hoisted one of them completely back into the building. His partner simply vanished into a billow of red smoke.

Barney materialized out of the riot of rainbow fog and pointed toward the door. None of them had uttered a syllable since the gate breach.

Inside they encountered minimal resistance. Sirius caught a frag from the wall in the forehead and instinctively returned fire with the shotgun. The orange smoke canister caught the shooter square in the noggin, almost somersaulting him backward. His MP5 skittered across the floor. As Barney stepped over him, he put a round in the guy's ear and the man stayed still.

If this was another wrong building, at least it was full of motivated hostiles with heavy ordnance. Nobody chopped so far could be deemed an innocent.

Barney located the elevator. They set it for the third floor, lobbed in a smoker, and moved for the stairs.

When they kicked through the stairway door on the second floor and deployed right-left-up-down, muzzles everywhere, a consternated sentry flung his pistol toward them and rabbitted away.

Long corridor, five rooms, max lock.

Barney held up his pinky finger, indicating flechettes

for the shotguns. Spiked brass rods instead of shot,
heavy powder, used by Feds to blow door hinges from
the outside. Sirius smoked the far end of the corridor
while Armand turned the first door to confetti. It was a
heavy wooden door, cross-barred, but once it lost its
hinges it sagged like an old prom queen. Inside a child
was screaming, balled into a wad in a far corner. No
leg shackle. Television. It was a little girl about eight,
her long hair beautiful but filthy, her coal-brown eyes
dilated in terror. Barney had to slap her lightly to get
her attention. "*Cuidado*," he said. "*Quedarse aqui,
nina. Regresamos inmediatamente; vamanos ahora.
¿Entiendes?*"

He had tried to say *watch out, stay here little girl,
we'll be right back, we're leaving today*. No doubt it
sounded like me-Tarzan you-Jane to the panicked girl,
but he did not want her running out into gunfire.
She seemed to grasp most of it and nodded, her eyes
shining with tears. He held her face with his mutilated
hand and made sure she registered the reassurance in
his own gaze. Then he pointed for her to stay right
where she was. "*¡Permaneces!*"

The alarm on his wristwatch peeped. Simultaneously, El Atrocidad's watch would be signaling, too.

It rains a great deal in Mexico City and its outback,
generally short bursts during midday in the wet season
—May through October on the *tierra fria*. It had rained
during Barney's first visit and no doubt had rained a lot
during his incarceration, although he had no memory
of hearing or smelling rainfall while he was shackled.
The rain, then, had not mattered or affected operations.
Outside the Palacio, now, it had begun to rain…

… which would not only cleanse the air for a scant
moment, it would also sabotage Barney's smokescreen.

They worked the corridor, smashing open the bolted doorways which held the latest crop of hostages. Another child, not Almirante. A beautiful, bedraggled woman in a miniskirt, no doubt snatched outside a club. A man who had lost a finger already and demanded a firearm so he could get involved. A woman who remained in her corner seat when the door flew down, and smiled when Barney looked at her, as though she had known all along he would arrive, perhaps in answer to a prayer.

Barney pointed. *Up.* Next floor.

Shooters on the third floor were ready to rumble, but ill-prepared for the smoke delivered by Sirius, squinting to see through the blood clogging his eye from his head wound. Armand took a rolling dive and managed to bracket the corridor, firing and reloading his .44. His hands were no longer shaking. Barney saw Karlov holster one firearm and execute a one-handed clip-change on another, smacking the fresh load against his knee and grimacing mostly for show. Sirius had his shotgun bowslung and was lopping the opposition apart a limb at a time shooting his twin Para-Ordnance semi-autos two-handed, walking and firing alternately, left-right-left-right. The slugs carved vapor trails through the thick green smoke, found targets, inflicted destruction.

Barney was slammed to the floor by two wild hits in the back, their killing penetration dispersed by the body armor, but their motive force burly enough to knock him on his face. He crawled to a locked door across the hall, grabbed the knob and fought to hoist himself upright. The breath had been punched out of his lungs and he needed to draw new air.

Sirius and Armand walked point, giving the hall

maximum coverage, expecting Barney and Karlov to follow in their wake to mop up by freeing the hostages on this floor.

Good god, how many people were held captive here? There were three more entire wings to the building.

Karlov handed over a shotgun and Barney blew the next door.

Instantly, gunfire erupted from within. Karlov snapped backward and fell down.

Through the dust and smoke as Barney ducked out of aimed sight, he glimpsed a naked man inside the room, emptying a big revolver at the intruders.

It was Zefir, the fat tormentor upon whom Barney had once puked, in another life. He had been interrupted in mid-rape by the invasion of the Palacio, but determined to achieve his wretched little squirt before his own special love-nest door wrenched apart into fiery splinters. Now he stood firing wild into the clouded green hallway, his pathetic erection barely visible in the shadow of his substantial belly. His victim was tied to a four-poster bed by athletic bandages and there was a game show blurring across the TV screen.

Barney fired with the shotgun from a distance of eight feet and the flechette round tore Zefir to ragged single-serve pieces. He actually glimpsed parts of his own body raining down around him before he dropped.

Karlov was attempting to sit up.

Barney saw this and watched long enough to see his comrade give a thumbs-up. *I'm okay, don't worry, move it!*

What was left of Zefir lay in a widening scarlet puddle on the wooden floor, his cognizance purely

reptilian. Barney slapped him to a semblance of aware-
ness, then hissed, "Sucio. *¿Donde está Sucio?*"

"*Gahhh*," said Zefir. He died.

Karlov limped into the breached room, favoring his
left leg. The woman on the bed had gone tharn while
being rompered by Zefir, and naturally reacted to his
intrusion as a preamble to further abuse. He had to
calm her down but could not muster much Spanish.

More gunfire, from the hallway. Mostly Armand and
Sirius, sweeping and clearing.

Barney handed the shotgun across, the message in
his eyes clear. *I'm going to follow them and open the
remaining rooms*. Karlov nodded just as the woman,
arms freed, grabbed him like a lost daughter and started
sobbing.

Other hostages were probably most secure in their
locked rooms until the floors could be flushed of gunners. Armand and Sirius knew they had to find the
room with the computers, the office of El Chingon.
They had zipped open enough rooms to verify they
were in the right place, doing the right thing.

Opposition began to wane noticeably. Gunners were
either dead or hightailing it.

Barney stepped out into the hallway to reload, and
that's when the enormous Sucio smashed into him like
a runaway bulldozer, grabbed him by the throat and
hefted him clear of the ground.

Thirty or more big-ticket hostages at $500 U.S. per day
was a rake of $15,000 every twenty-four hours—not
bad when you considered it was above and beyond the
ransom demands, which corkscrewed up into the millions more often than you would assume possible, given

Mexico's reputation as one of the world's great sink-holes of poverty. Tannenhauser had a wonderful little slot machine going at the Palacio; it nearly always paid off. Tannenhauser was the man Barney wanted. Sucio was the man he got.

Sucio, the stone-idol sonofabitch who had snipped off Barney's fingers, then forced them down Barney's throat. Sucio, who had the blood-rage for the death of his brother Jesús at the hands of a pair of *pinche gringos*. Sucio, of the daily beatings and humiliation, head pervert of the guard branch of this madhouse. The man who had shot Barney four times and dumped his carcass into the sewer, albeit not in that order.

He was a year older, a year more aromatic, and his gouged eye had healed into a droop that mocked Tannenhauser's lazy left orb. He emerged from the green fog like the legendary *chupacabra*, neckless, fulminating with anger, the size of a small bear. That make-believe bloodsucking cryptid, brother to Sasquatch and the Abominable Snowman, was said to possess the power to give mortals nausea with its glowing red eyes. Sucio pretty much fit the profile.

Barney had rehearsed this moment a half-million times in his mind. He would track Sucio down, cripple him, make sure he knew who was killing him, and then finish him off, maybe after making him eat all of his own fingers. Or Barney would shoot him in the legs with his .22 until Sucio would gladly chop off his own penis to escape the pain. Something that was the ultimate in degradation. Barney would taunt the bigger man, spitting his venom back at him, trying for some humiliation that could compensate for what Barney had lost. But no matter what he did to Sucio, the only thing it would change was whether or not Sucio still occupied the world of the living. Payback ran deeper than that.

It was all an indulgent joke, anyway, with Barney as the butt. Because Sucio had appeared out of nowhere instead of being tracked and run to ground. He now had Barney's neck in a vise-grip and was crushing his larynx. And in the big man's face was no sign of recognition at all. None.

And now Barney was going to die by Sucio's hand not far from the first Bleeding Room; joke squared.

Barney's gun thumped to the floor at Sucio's feet. Barney's legs kicked and thrashed. No good.

Sucio increased the pressure with his weightlifter muscle. Hydrostatics would blast Barney's eyes from his head like pimentos from olives. The world washed scarlet. Sucio was going to tweeze his head completely free of his body with the sound of a popped pimple.

Air was a memory as Barney struggled to breathe. Drowning, again.

Sucio flinched but kept Barney in his deathgrip. Flinched twice more. In delayed molasses-time, Barney vaguely registered the sound of gunshots. Twice more. Gradually the hammerlock on his esophagus eased back, just a notch.

Again. Again.

Karlov was sitting on the floor of the hostage room, legs out in front of him, wavering but accurately delivering the payload of his unholstered .357 into Sucio's back one round at a time. Sucio dropped to one knee, still clutching Barney's neck. Still twitching from hits. Barney's swimming vision made dim sense of Armand, standing in the hallway, calmly aiming, firing, and walking closer with each round. Beside him, Sirius took alternate shots, adding more lead to Sucio's body fat index. When the giant killer finally released Barney and slumped, Barney saw the heel of the Army .45 sticking out of his waistband—the old Colt 1911-A Barney had picked up cheap for the original ransom run, the one Sucio had taken from him.

Barney sprawled on his side, gasping, his eyes staying on the gun even though his vision was hazed and occluded. Or had Sirius let off another grenade? Didn't matter. *Put your hand on that pistol.*

Still sucking draughts of oxygen laced with green smoke, Barney pulled the .45 free of Sucio's pants. Sucio was trying to crabwalk himself toward the far wall, his metabolism blowing fuses, his blood flooding out to soak the floor.

Barney snapped the action of the semi-auto to chamber his first *thank you* to the man who had meant so much to him.

After steadying himself against the wall, Barney pushed off like a swimmer and emptied the magazine into Sucio's chest at point blank range.

Contrary to entrenched cliché and what nitwits repeatedly say on the evening news, shots do not "ring out," and anybody who tells you they do has never heard gunfire. Report is more akin to the startlement of a heavy door slammed by a gust of wind; you know how *that* makes you jump, and no matter how prepared you think you are, the sound always comes as a surprise. It stops time for a millisecond and obliterates all other sound. Ignition and launch of a bullet evacuates the air from around your head in a phenomenon called blowback. If you're not ready for it, the noise jump-starts the human fight-or-flight reflex in some small primitive corner of the brain. You freeze momentarily until the gunshot allows the rest of the world to come back. Once you've gotten past that first shot, subsequent shots are easy—you can even make them without blinking because your mind has processed that initial speed-stop, which no way, nohow, never in history, "rings out."

Pink, frothy lung-blood was slobbering from Sucio's mouth. Barney could see the tiny lights in the man's eyes, fading to black.

Blood was coursing from both of Barney's hands, oozing past the snugs on the shooting gloves. His new hands would always be limited in certain ways. But they could still give Sucio the finger, which was the last thing he saw before he died.

Then the corridor filled up with shouting men in Mexican wrestling masks, and Barney knew the cavalry had arrived.

Karlov was dead.

He had breathed his last after pumping the final rounds of his .357 into Sucio, from where he had slumped on the floor of the room with the naked lady in it. His body armor had shielded him from all the hits in the hallway except for the one wild, heavy-caliber shot from Zefir, which angled in by sheer chance to slam his femoral artery so hard that it ruptured beneath the skin. All the time he was calming the rape victim, helping Barney, and holding up his end of the assault, he was hemorrhaging, and he finally ran dry. Internal bleeding left his leg completely black.

Their guns were literally too hot to holster.

Barney's plan was to alert El Atrocidad and his men as soon as the assault commenced. By the time they could rally and storm the Palacio, the shooting would be done…and the masked superstars of lucha libre could take credit for rescuing thirty or more hostages. It should have come as no surprise that the wrestlers were standing by and eager to jump; they showed up early by Barney's wristwatch, and got to pound a few criminal heads in the deal. The most astonishing part was that they showed up in costume—flamboyant spandex, filigreed masks and boots for stomping. A couple had sequined capes. Flecha de Jalisco was wearing a gray business suit and tie, but with the sleeves ripped off due to his gunshot wound. These men were accustomed to fighting in their sacred masks, and barreled into the Palacio practically foaming to take on all comers with a hysterical bravery that would make you think it was a pay-per-view event.

Armand had discovered Flecha's son Almirante locked in a third floor room, west wing. The boy's fingers were all intact. One more day and the merch might have devalued enough for the kidnappers to begin lopping parts.

Some bad guy stragglers caught the worst of it, getting flung two stories down, hammered until they were raw meat, or centered in a kicking contest by two or three luchadors. No way this fighting was fake, and the blood was more real than ever.

All the masked men thought Barney was *el campeon de justicia*, and Atrocidad told him so.

"But that is not the reason you do this." El Atrocidad winked at Barney from the depths of his green, vinyl-flamed mask, his grin like a grille, his face like the front end of a Chevy low-rider. "The champion of justice, that is part of the lucha libre *leyendo*, the legend. You do this thing and want no one to know it is you, except those you punish."

"I'm no hero," said Barney. His throat was still scoured and aching. Breathing hurt. "I've killed unarmed men. I've lied and bushwhacked them for no other reason than revenge."

"You might think that," said Atrocidad. "You might even talk yourself into believing it. But I know better. You came back to Mexico for a right reason, *correcto, ¿no?*"

There would never be any way to explain it to the big goateed man.

If El Atrocidad was exuberant, Flecha de Jalisco was gushing, effusive, verging on tears, and who was Barney to say the man's gratitude was not deep and genuine? He had reclaimed his son from the forces of evil men. But Barney could not take much more gruff good cheer in the name of justice.

What now? During the mop-up, everybody looked to Barney as though he was some kind of leader, and all Barney could look at was the lifeless form of his good friend Karlov, lost thanks to his vendetta.

"Now?" said Barney. "What now? We get the hell outta Dodge before the news trucks show up. But first we have to give them a show. Once El Atrocidad and his men get the hostages clear, we burn this fucking place to the ground, to ashes. If Tannenhauser isn't here, then there's nothing left. His scumbag army are all dead or fled. One thing—I want to find the room. *The* room. The burning starts there."

"Yeah, well before you go all pyromaniacal on us," said Sirius, "I've got a guy handcuffed to a water pipe up on Three you might want to have a word with. Over next to the computer room."

Barney just wanted to sleep. Post-combat metabolic flush, when your adrenalin has cooked away, is opiate in its draining effect. Sirius told him more, but it washed over Barney, who clumped along, unhearing.

Seeing the guy Sirius had detained woke Barney up doublequick.

"Saaay, amigo!" said the battered man braceleted to the immovable pipework. "It's you! They kill you and you don't die, eh? Or are you *el espectro*, a ghost come to visit his havoc on earth? *Amigo!* What a pleasure to see you!"

"Mojica," said Barney. "You're Mojica."

"Aha, see?!" The shaved dome of the too-fervent, murine man was leaking nervous sweat. His trademark mirrorshades were trampled on the floor. "Remember I told you I help you get out? And you got out! You remember me, eh? You remember that I help you so this *maricon* don't shoot me?" His introduction to Sirius had not been amicable.

"I'll shoot you myself," said Barney, "if you don't tell me where El Chingon is. Tannenhauser. Whatever that stick-up-the-ass animal calls himself."

The entire front of Sirius' face crumpled together in a frown. "You *know* this dude?"

"Just an acquaintance," said Barney.

"O-ha, you kid, you kid!" said Mojica with false bluster. "That is the big joke, my friend, the biggest joke of all: El Chingon had to go to America. Come on, you can laugh, guy, it's funny! He had some bigshot

El Chingon business in *Los Estados Unidos*. He's not even fucking *here*, *ese!* And I tell you sure as shit he's not coming back now, not after you—" he searched for the right words "—*redecorated* this place, eh?"

"This little rodent pulled a nine on me," said Sirius.

"You look okay," said Barney.

"No worries."

Mojica looked despondent. His chances sucked and he knew it. "So…you gonna kill me now?" He tried for a hopeful-puppy expression that was vomitous.

"I'll do it," said Sirius, unsleeving his .45.

"Wait," said Barney.

That was all Mojica needed to recharge his battery, and during the next few seconds he was as obsequious as it is possible for a human being to be without actually devolving into a lower life form. Barney had to smack him to shut him up.

"Listen very carefully," Barney said. "*Escuchame bien*. You tell me where he is. Where he has gone; where I can find him, not later, not maybe, not eventually, but right now. You tell me that, Mojica, and you'll not only live, but you'll go free, right now, tonight. And if you're lying to me in any way, I will come back here just for the pleasure of taking your life in the most painful and drawn-out way I can conceive. Think about that, before you answer."

"You remembered my name," the little man said, quietly.

"I try to remember everybody who kicks the piss out of me. Helps at Christmas card time." Mojica had sterilized his amputated fingers—his face floated up out of the dim cesspool of pain-memory. Mojica had done him one small kindness during his days of torment. That bought him some wiggle room, but did not forgive his other sins.

Maybe Mojica *had* helped Barney escape, if by no other way than not shooting him when Sucio did following Barney's bridge dive, headfirst and with no form at all.

It was so easy to be seduced by the thought. Conned, tricked, made a stupid mark, yet again.

Sirius centered Barney in his gaze: *We can't let this guy go. Not after—*

Barney imagined what Karlov might have said: *For a man on the revenge trail you sure are sparing a lot of warm bodies.*

And Armand: *You cut him loose now, he'll be a problem later. Not professional.*

Against all this stood Mojica's one little favor he had not had to do, but had done anyway.

"Los Angeles," Mojica said. "He's with that guy's, your friend's, you know, that redheaded *puta*. Your guy's wife."

There was much more detail and Barney ran Mojica through the repetition wringer to ensure the tale was not cobbled on the spot. In the end, Mojica sang like a crested warbler just for being uncuffed before Barney's crew set the Palacio to the torch.

Barney stood in the empty room where he had once been held prisoner.

It was apparently the only room outfitted for problematical detainees. Real hostages got amenities— locked in, not chained up. Beds and television, though the beds were probably lice-infested, and if you need a quick way to go gibberingly crazy there was no quicker method than watching a lot of foreign TV.

Barney wished he could feel some surge of latent emotion, but the room had given up its haunts. It was just a depressing, empty space .

El Atrocidad appeared behind him, moving lightly with his big athlete's grace. "Not all people in Mexico are like this, amigo," he said softly.

"You've done far too much for me, for far too little return," said Barney. "I'm in your debt. I always will be. There's no way to repay… This is unusual for me."

El Atrocidad made a *chaa* sound of dismissal. *It ain't no thing.* "Look at what you have accomplished. Look at the people you have saved."

"I didn't do it to save them."

"Evil men dealt with."

"It won't make any difference tomorrow."

"You even give all the *credito* to us."

"Take it. I don't want it."

"Then what do you want from this?"

"My friend back in the hall. His name is Christoph Ivan Karlov. I need you to take him out of here. He needs to be buried. I don't think he would mind being buried in Mexico."

He imagined Karlov's response: *I don't care, young-ster—I'm dead. You gave me the challenge of showing a man with crippled hands how to shoot again. You put my weapons in the hands of true gunmen. You gave me plenty. You don't owe me nothing. Just get on with the mission, damn it.*

"El Murcielago Sangriento tells me the news people are on their way," someone said.

Armand brought up a gallon of gasoline from some-where in the compound, and Barney splashed it around the Bleeding Room. Ignited it. Walked away. Within minutes the entire third floor was ablaze.

The Palacio burned for five hours, due to difficulties with firefighting response and a lack of local water pressure. News cameras loved fire, and only later got around to the poignant report of rescued hostages. The wrestlers got a lot of face time, explaining they were en route to a match as a group and spotted the flames. Their next bout at Arena Coliseo would be packed and they would he hailed as superheroes, some of the best Mexico had to offer.

When the conflagration embered down, even the brickwork had fallen, sundered by the collapsing interior of the building. By dawn the next day the site resembled the aftermath of a bombing, or just another run-down Mexican firetrap gone to its reward. The news of a fire in a shithole like Iztapalapa was not important enough to make the papers in the United States, and besides, nobody would believe that stuff about strongmen in circus-colored costumes giving a crowd of people their lives back.

For all intents and purposes, Barney and his men had never been there.

Part Four
Felt Recoil

What the desperate Mojica had been able to provide was a key phone number, a last resort backup, emergencies only. Which number, when properly traced, could serve as a homing beacon for a stakeout location in Los Angeles. Barney already knew what his targets looked like. He had Tannenhauser's dictatorial mien imprinted on his memory. As for Erica—whatever she was calling herself these days—he had Carl Ledbetter's wallet photo.

It was enough.

Armand and Sirius were spoiling for more, especially since the loss of Karlov, whose burial had been private, in an undisclosed location. Barney, stung by this post facto price on his mission, was reluctant to place his remaining allies in the path of harm. Progress choked, once they had returned home to lives and existences that seemed even more pointless after the blood-fever of battle. Barney told them he had to be very careful, time would be needed to make extremely discreet inquiry and follow-up, and that he would flag them the moment he had his final two targets.

Barney was, of course, lying.

Based on a bit of sublegal cellular tracking, it was necessary to isolate Tannenhauser's signal as soon as possible, since the man would be on the move as soon as the import of the disaster in Mexico resonated.

Since you could never lop off every head of a Hydra, Barney assumed Tannenhauser would be apprised immediately—so he had to fob off Sirius and Armand and land on this man's tail mega-quick.

He had staked out the Sheraton Miramar in Santa Monica for a whole day, tracking comings and goings. He had spotted Tannenhauser once, and seen a woman who might have been the former Erica Ledbetter three times, depending on how she could have changed her look over the past two years.

They appeared to be together, as Mojica had said.

Just today, outside, waiting for a car, they had appeared to be arguing.

Now all Barney had to do was time them out, and tag them inside the building. Figuring out what code names they were registered under was a waste of time. He had them and they did not appear to be anxious to relocate just yet. There was probably a lot of long-distance spin control going on, the kind that was safer to do from another country.

He would scoop them alone, and his men might be spared a stray bullet.

Armand ruined all of Barney's quiet strategy with a single cellphone call.

"You've got to get down here now."

Bad news, incoming, take cover…

"Somebody nailed Sirius. Right outside the gun range. Wherever you go, don't go back there because I'm pretty sure it's hot. Meet me at the morgue, four o'clock."

The downtown Los Angeles County Department of the Coroner—the county morgue, due west of the University of Southern California Medical Center—

has a gift shop on its second floor called Skeletons in the Closet, where one can buy "ghoulish gifts" such as toe tag keyrings, coffee mugs featuring a body outline in chalk, or toy miniatures of the 1938 Black Mariah hearse. Profits from the shop go to stout causes such as the Youthful Drunk Driving Visitation Program, which, among other incentives to reform, compels offenders to watch an actual autopsy-in-progress. Founded in 1993, the shop pulls down between $15,000 and $20,000 in sales every month (excepting, of course, Halloween season, when it does double that) and has an international clientele.

People who visit the morgue for the purposes of putting a name to a corpse usually don't stop at the gift shop for a souvenir.

The late Sirius had a small-caliber bullet hole straight through his head. You could actually see through it; blow frigid condensed breath through it, if you had the guts to lift it from the confines of the body bag on refrigerated drawer-tray Number 38.

"They're hunting us," said Armand. "We're not as smart or cool as we thought we were. We destroyed their operation in Mexico and now the sonofabitch is going to pick us off locally. The only reason he missed you is because you've spent so much time staking out the hotel. Me, I can't figure. We might walk out of here and right into a gunsight."

"I know where he is," said Barney.

"Then we take him. Sudden death overtime." Armand nailed his friend eye-to-eye. "I know what you're going to try to sell me. You're going to say the hunt is over, that this isn't Mexico, that it's *your* problem. Then, when I don't believe that, you're going to say it's not worth it. They hired a guy to kill you in Mexico when you were slightly less mobile than a rutabaga, and they're going to keep hiring soldiers until we are dust. You and me are the same, now—our dead friend in the drawer there is proof positive."

"I was going to suggest you go hole up with your brother in Cincinnati until the gunsmoke clears."

"Let history pass me by? Fuck that."

Sirius' dead, closed eyes offered them no counsel. No one else was present to waste time by suggesting *maybe it was all an accident, random, unrelated, a tragedy, sure, but nothing more*.

"You've got the bloodlust, partner," Armand said. "Keep it boiling and don't let it blind you to tactical reality."

"Armand," Barney said. "I let one go in New York City. I shouldn't have. I let one go in Mexico and I shouldn't have. But each one was a negotiative play for a bigger target. It's me that Tannenhauser wants; let me take the risk. I don't want you getting waxed now that Karlov and Sirius are gone."

"I'm a big boy," said Armand. "Practically a grown-up." He waited a beat. Barney was not smiling. "All or nothing."

They left the morgue. No place was safe. The person who had killed Sirius had walked right up to him, put a pistol to his temple, and fired.

Barney flexed his hands, trying to remember what they had looked like when they were whole.

"You're right. This isn't over until they're all gone." Grimly he thought, *Or we are*.

Their entire arsenal—what they had not disposed of in Mexico—was trapped at the gun range, inacces-

sible. It was tainted ground until they were clear.
Barney had his Super .40 and Armand had his Ruger,
end of story. It would be so easy to hit the freeway and
keep on driving. This was not home anymore.

"See, now that wasn't so hard, was it?" said Armand,
slapping his friend on the shoulder.

"We just jump in the car, drive to the hotel, kill
some people and then have a steak dinner?"

Armand remote-fobbed the doors on his ride, a low,
gorgeous Cadillac DTS V-8 in pewter. "No. We jump
in the car, drive to the hotel, smoke the snake-in-the-
grass motherfuckers that subtracted Sirius from our
lives, and *then* go have a steak dinner. Chez Jay's. I'll
buy. Our dead buddy in there needs one toast at least."

Yes. At least. At least in a couple of hours it would
all be done…

Barney was nearly at peace with that brutal truth
when Armand grinned at him over the roof of the car.
Then everything behind Armand's ears burst toward
Barney in a macerated mist of red blood, white bone,
gray brains.

Barney walloped his chin on the car roof in his hurry
to hit the deck, saturated in the remains of the back of
Armand's head. Armand collapsed in a boneless
tumble. Two seconds ago, this had not happened yet.

Another .338 Lapua round pierced the door on
Armand's side and exited through Barney's door three
inches from his head. It was a flat trajectory. The
shooter was so far away that the echo of distant report
came after the bullet had struck. These were boat-
tailed, full metal jacketed military rounds, Super Mag-
nums with a muzzle energy of nearly five thousand

foot-pounds. This was the sort of death you got at the
hands of an expert with a four thousand-dollar rifle
and painfully precise optics. The guy could be 1500
meters away. Anywhere.

Barney had about two feet of clearance he was
pretty sure the shooter could not aim below. Clawing
his own gun out would have been pointless. This was
surgical, dispassionate, the slaughter of farm animals.

He crawled on his belly toward a palm tree plant-
er made out of UltraCal while several more rounds
chopped and channeled Armand's car. It was absurdly
quiet. There was a good chance the sniper had not
seen him move.

Barney actually heard the whine of the incoming
slug cutting air. A cloud of gasified fiber turned the air
yellow and the palm tree fell over like a British butler,
bowing.

Even if he could make it back to the car, what was
the point? There was probably a bullet deep in the
engine block by now.

Sirius had been killed at the gun range, and the
enemy had figured Barney and Armand would come
to the morgue. The question that might save Barney's
life was: Had the sniper seen Barney's car?

It was parked on the other side of the street, a
leased Dodge Hemi Charger in gunmetal gray. The
only armament it offered was one of Karlov's Benellis,
in the trunk along with some spare ammo for the .40.
Both useless.

*It stinks, amigo. It stinks like underbrush when you
probe by fire.*

Carl's words from an eternity ago echoed back at
him. That's what this superior sonofabitch was doing,

but from a leisurely bench rest. He probably had time to sip a Primer Pop between rounds until it was time for him to pack up, drive away, and eat his own god-damned steak.

Nothing left to do. No options.

Barney unholstered his .40 and put five rounds through the windows in front of the morgue, aiming high, hoping not to hit anybody. The sheet glass caved in with a breathtaking racket, people screamed, hollered and sought cover, alarms sounded, and pretty soon there would be police swarming.

Barney crawled toward his car, hands and knees the whole way, cringing at honking traffic.

After parking on Ocean Boulevard and punching the steering wheel a few times to vent his backlog of adrenalin, Barney refreshed his SIG Sauer and walked toward the hotel entrance, where he spotted Erica Ledbetter crossing the lobby in a brisk hurry.

She coded as feminine right down to the ground: attractive ankles, hell on heels, calves with the precise roundness to stop traffic at a leg crossing, the classic hourglass, real hips. She lacked the insectile height of fashion models, but put her in a bikini magazine spread where height is a digitally enhanced mystery and all you'd ever notice were those soft-shoulder, dangerous-when-wet curves. Her padding was all to her advantage and she lacked the bovine look of women who fret about dress size. This woman never fretted about anything. You could read her determination in the precise cut of jaw, the elegant neck, the eyes so blue they hurt to look at, like pure cyan broken off the sun's spectrum and laser-refracted through a crystal. She was the woman Barney had seen in Carl's photograph, but distilled into something more fierce.

She walked like a woman with a mission, and Barney managed to trap her in the elevator, alone.

"Wow, I always wanted a new man in my life, and voila," she said, startled yet not surprised. "I'll assume that's a gun in my ribs, and not that you're happy to see me."

"Overjoyed," said Barney. "Stay in the corner. Hold the rails. Bag on the floor."

Now she was looking at him directly. "You're him," she said. "Carl's guy."

From the bag Barney extracted a ten-shot, Black Melonite-coated Cobra Patriot in .380. He quickly popped the magazine. Three rounds gone.

It might have been any of them walking into the kill zone back at the gun range, but Sirius had drawn the duty. The hole in his head had not come from a guy with a four thousand dollar rifle, but someone who got close enough to shoot point-blank, perhaps with this pistol.

The illuminated numerals crawled toward the fourth floor. "What do I call you?" said Barney.

"Who cares?" she said. "What's in a name?"

She fostered dislike, but apparently did not care, even with a gun pointed at her. She was far too attractive to be smiling at her captor now and saying, "It's nice to meet you at last," as though they were headed for a high school reunion. She should have had hazard tape on her forehead, and Barney was acutely aware of a completely different kind of arsenal coming into play.

"If you have any sort of special knock, or code, don't

break it to warn him," said Barney, meaning Tannenhauser. "If there is gunfire, lady, you are going to be point number one, I swear it."

"Whatever," she said, as though this had all been rehearsed. Her sheer indifference was disorienting.

He swept the hall. No bystanders.

"Oh, the *drama*," she said. "It's not necessary. Listen, Tannenhauser is not going to shoot you. I promise."

Barney indicated she should use her key card and walk through first anyway.

They were top floor in one of the Miramar's biggest suites, and she strolled in on those fabulous legs as though she owned a controlling interest in the hotel.

"Slow down," Barney said.

"*Relax*," she returned. "Look, I did not kill your friend." She headed for a fully stocked roll-in cocktail counter that must have billed at a good $1200.

"Sit in the chair right there."

"And stay?" she said impishly. "*Woof*. I am going to fix myself a drink for our little talk. You're welcome to one too, but I don't expect you'll take one and relax."

She set about concocting a bourbon and branch water while Barney stared at her. "This isn't some kind of goddamned *meeting*, lady," he said.

"Yes it is," she said. "A meeting. You'll see."

Barney half-expected Tannenhauser to saunter out in a smoking jacket with a martini, to deliver an opening line like *Gentlemen, I'm sure we can clear up this little misunderstanding*…before attempting to buy, bribe, lie or kill his way clear.

The bedroom double doors were open and the curtains drawn. Dark inside. Feet in silk socks, no shoes, dangled from the king bed.

Tannenhauser—El Chingon—was spreadeagled across the down comforter, one tiny bloodsmear on the fabric and three bullet holes in his chest, a compact and lethal shot group. Both his eyes matched now, gazing sightlessly in two different directions. The tip of his tongue protruded from his slack lips. He had not been dead for very long, his body still cooling, courting rigor mortis.

She stirred her drink and kept her seat. "Now can we talk?"

"I guess he outlived his usefulness, too," Barney said. "Like all of them—Felix Rainer, Carl…me."

She made a dismissive gesture with her glass. "Felix was a nervous, impotent little paranoid that needed adventurous solutions. Carl was a loser looking to win the lottery." She indicated the bedroom, where Tannenhauser had not yet been dead an hour. "He was …greedy. And kind of nasty. He was going to kill you himself when you got here, did you know that part?"

There was no place in the room where Barney could be comfortable holding a gun on this woman. There was no place on the planet where he could be comfortable even being near her. He felt an irretrievable black-mamba vibe warning him to stay sharp. She was too reassuring, too easy to look at, and he should just add lead to her diet and hustle away. But uncannily, she seemed to sense his need to know things. Radar was one of her primary weapons.

She made a little frown and continued: "After his man killed your friend—I forget which one—Tannenhauser knew you'd come here. I think his vile little plan was to kill me, then you, wrap us up, and get out." She shrugged. "I changed the plan."

Gun Work   231

"You fucked them all," Barney said with unconscious marvel.

"I don't know that who I sleep with has anything to do with anything," she said with false outrage.

"You know what I mean."

"Yes, well…" She shrugged; no biggie. "Tanny was a greedy entrepreneur looking for the next big score. He and Carl and Felix were like one personality split up into three parts. Putting them together was obvious."

"You mean playing them off of each other."

"Semantics. I put them together and the deal invented itself. I don't vouch for the workability of it."

"Meaning: you were clean no matter what happened."

"Now you're getting it."

"All you had to do was seduce each of them."

She emitted a *pffffhht* sound of annoyance. "All I did was utilize the chemistry. You're big enough to have learned there's no such thing as romance, right? It's all DNA. Romance and love are the window dressing with which we tart up our vulgar biology; we use it to excuse our animal hungers in an attempt to delude ourselves that we are some sort of higher being. We're not, you know." She narrowed her eyes at him even as the pheromones flew off her skin like mustard gas. "You do know that, yes?"

"I know about black widow spiders," said Barney. "I know about the preying mantis, chomping the head off the male after sex."

"You see? This is the problem: People get all judgmental about nature. There's no right or wrong in nature. That's a human conceit."

"You mean nature as in eat-or-get-eaten. You eat

men like Felix and Carl. You consume what you need, shit them out, and move on to your next victim. Sometimes the bodies you leave in your wake aren't even all the way dead."

"Those men were more alive with me than they had ever been. I didn't force them to do anything they didn't already want to do."

"That's very orderly, but it's not the truth."

"Why don't you tell me what the truth is?"

"The truth is you found men with weaknesses and aimed them at each other. You set up the operation so they would eliminate each other when their usefulness was spent."

"Seems to me *you* eliminated most of them."

"Yes. I'm the biggest sucker of all. I got conned into this with the best of intentions. You were the one who made sure I would suffer enough that I'd want retribution, enough to justify whatever retribution I could muster. And I did it, just like clockwork. Wind me up and watch me shoot. I did it for me — but each step was at your direction. And to your profit." The symmetry of the deception was an awesome thing to behold in the light.

"Why didn't you kill Felix?" she said.

"I didn't have to. Felix will kill himself. That much was obvious. He'll flame out, get caught, or otherwise compromise himself. He doesn't need anybody to kill him. Sorry I messed up the perfection of your hit list."

"You didn't kill Felix, but you did kill Carl."

"I thought Carl was the main viper in this snakepit. I made a mistake."

"Aww, how sweet—you killed him for *betraying* you. Very macho. You're such a *man*, aren't you? It takes a lot of guts to murder someone that ready to die, doesn't it?" She sipped her drink. The look of satisfaction, of satiation on her face was enough to make Barney wish he could kill her more than once.

"How long are you going to drag this out?" Barney said.

"I've got all the time in the world," she said. "So do you. I'm enjoying this, and you could too, if you'd just have a drink and relax."

Her expression, Barney realized, was the one she probably wore while eating up cockfights or pit-bull tournaments. The face with which corrupt Romans watched speared gladiators, or biowar scientists regarded little designer germs reproducing. Not pleasant.

"Turn-down service might be a little upset to find a corpse in the room," said Barney. "No extra chocolate mint." Barney could not see her angle. Time was ticking away. What sort of out did she think she had?

"Oh, I see—you think if you can antagonize me, I'll do something rash. Like charge you in a flurry of high heels and perfume and die a sort of film noir death? Sorry. I'm not built that way. Tell me: What happened to Mister Moraine?"

Barney's expression told her it was a mystery.

"The blond man Tannenhauser hired to take care of you in Mexico. We had to outsource him; he cost a lot of money."

Click; recognition. Once Tannenhauser was in the saddle with Erica and Carl had been subtracted, it was child's play for him to check emergency rooms all over the continent after Barney's escape, or rather, disposal. *Click*; the *clinica*. *Click*; Dr. Mendez dies after giving up Barney. The imported assassin dies at Mano's house...

DAVID J. SCHOW

... and *click*; the plan changes. Barney is left alone, allowed to live, because what has been done to him is so monstrous that he will do Erica the favor of erasing Felix (*oops*), erasing Carl (*check*), and cleaning up the Palacio, thereby erasing every footprint that could lead back to Erica. But Erica is stuck with Tannenhauser, who has all the money. Tannenhauser does not get killed in Mexico. But he does the next best thing: He comes to America to join up with Erica under a totally bogus identity, on the run from the crazy gunman who is, according to intel, back in Mexico behind a huge boner of payback and terminating everybody involved in hurting him. According to every register, credit card bill and travel itinerary, Tannenhauser is not in Los Angeles, which makes him especially easy to eliminate a la carte and at sole discretion.

"He got killed," said Barney of the wordless Mr. Moraine.

"Now you're getting it. You killed him before he could kill you—very honorable."

And as the Palacio had burned, that dirtbag Mojica had scampered to the nearest phone to give Tannenhauser the heads-up. *Here he comes.*

Still, Mojica had been as good as his corrupt word. Barney's deal was: *Tell me where I can find Tannenhauser; do not lie, and you shall go free.* Mojica had abided by those terms, which did not prevent him from alerting Tannenhauser. Damn it all, the little weasel had played *fair.*

"Who killed Sirius?"

Erica's forehead crinkled. "Who killed who?"

"My partner. At the shooting range."

"Oh, the bald man? Sorry, bub; no chance for justice

there. After Moraine blew it, Tannenhauser decided
to actually work, for a change. He had all you guys
tracked the second you stepped back into LA. Tanny
had enough spine to do the first, but had to hire the
second, because he knew you guys would be spooked.
More needless expense."

Armand had smiled, then died, right in front of
Barney. *Needless expense.*

"Don't you get it?" she said. "There's no call for all
this hairy, erect, masculine gun-waving. Tanny was
going to kill you when you showed here, not me—
because I'd already be dead. I shot him with that little
gun you found in my purse. It was easy, and a little bit
exciting." Almost independently, her left hand had
gone down to stroke the inside of her thigh, as though
she was experiencing a rush from the recent memory
of murder.

"Felix Rainer was in the process of giving me the
heave-ho," she continued. "I was just a boring little
employee at a fashion magazine. He was abusive. Carl
saved me—he really did."

"That's not the way Carl told it." Barney recalled
the epic story of Rafe Torgeson, another presumed
abuser from whom Erica needing saving.

"There were a couple of bad choices in between,"
she said. "But I knew enough to put Carl and Felix in
the same room together. Their scheme hatched itself.
It was just as likely to implode as succeed, but in the
process a lot of cash would be floating around. One
day Carl said he had known a fellow in Iraq, a brother
in arms, the kind of guy about whom you say, 'Gee, I
wish he was here; he could solve everything.' The kind
of man who would make a good enforcer, and in the

process, increase the odds of a scam actually working to everybody's profit. That would be you. All I had to do was encourage Carl to phone you up. But a polite social cocktail-party solicitation was not the way. From what Carl said, I guessed you would respond to a crisis, and I guessed correctly, didn't I? The late Mr. Tannenhauser was the first to see the potential cash-flow possibilities as a satellite to his kidnapping racket, which was already thriving. When you surprised everybody by surviving, it became clear that the whole chain-of-title could be erased, which is always nice when great gobs of money are concerned. That bloodbath in Mexico? I didn't do that. You did it. Case fucking *closed*." She seemed to deflate at the possibility it was all beyond Barney. "Look, do I have to drag a blackboard and a pointer in here?"

"The only thing left," said Barney, "is money. Enough to fight over. Enough to cause problems later. How much did Tannenhauser have when he left Mexico?"

"Oh, a second ago you wanted to kill me and now you want to talk money."

"You put me and my friends in harm's way, and right now I am the only one left standing. I got shot. Mutilated. Hospitalized. My friends died around me."

"Please. Who recruited them? You did. Hence, they are dead because of what you did—your little revenge mission. Feel better, yes or no? Besides, I think your hands are rather elegant." She fingered an expensive jade choker on her equally expensive neck. "May I see them without those gloves?"

"No. What happened to the money?"

She exhaled nasally, piqued at this talk of money when she would rather be involved in a seduction. "Five million, in three cases, in the bedroom. That works out to a bit more than a million and a half per case, and change. Take any one of them. And go, if you're going to be dull. Take one for your trouble, and consider yourself fortunate." She flitted her hands at him. "Go on; they're not short-count or booby-trapped or anything."

Barney did not move.

A tiny line of frustration creased her brow. "Oh, come *on*," she said. "Don't tell me you haven't fantasized about fucking me. Especially if I am so goddamned dangerous. Men like you are addicted to risk, and risking your life makes you horny, don't bother to deny it. You and I are survivors; we are the last people standing. That's why I wanted to meet you. That's why we have all the time in the world. The war is *over*, lover. You could forget the gun-waving and penetrate me with something better than a bullet, and it would be worth it. I guarantee it. I've been looking forward to it as much as you have." She was stimulating herself with her own speech, going lubricious right there in the chair. "Or you can be a bore and just take your little suitcase of money and split…and wonder for the rest of your life what it would have been like."

She really was a consummate businesswoman, except for one infinitesimal detail.

"What's to stop me from taking them all?" said Barney.

In response, she laughed. It was a fluting sound, rich and sonorous, the kind of laugh that could make royalty sacrifice a kingdom. "Oh, doll…"

Then from out of nowhere she leveled a Charter Arms Bulldog at him and smooched a quartet of .44-caliber rounds right into his chest.

Part Five
Blowback

She was leaning over him to check for blood when he grabbed her by the throat. She was so shocked she actually dropped the Bulldog revolver, which had one round left in its cylinder.

They were all here, Barney thought. Karlov, Armand, Sirius. He was wearing Karlov's gloves and special neck strap. The ammo in his gun's magazine had been manufactured by Armand. And Sirius had supplied the floppy green body armor he wore under his clothing, which had just spared his life.

He felt as though he had been kicked in the solar plexus by a Clydesdale, then run over by a semi, then dragged. His vision was aswim and he was unable to sit up yet. But he'd managed a lock on her beautiful neck, and he'd die before he'd let go.

She clawed his face open with lacquered nails, white foam actually accreting at the corners of her mouth. This was her real face, the face nobody ever saw, the visage beneath the human mask, her cunning mimic of human behavior.

She tried to roundhouse him in the balls, something the body armor was not specifically designed to prohibit. He lunged. They rolled. She went for an eye gouge and he feinted, feeling his ear tear halfway off. Then she spotted his .40 on the floor—much closer than where her Bulldog had fallen—and made a wide, swinging grab for it in spite of his chokehold. Barney's face went right into the valley of her perfect breasts. Her porcelain skin was trying to push its scent right into his brain.

So he bit her.

It was a grotesque parody of sex: her bucking and gasping as though she was coming her brains out, skirt hiked up past her waist, knees straddling him; him red-faced and straining, thrusting against her, his face buried in her cleavage. Barney's teeth clamped down on soft tissue and tore free a wet, crimson mouthful which he spat out. She did not scream. She was not a screamer. The sound that burst from her was closer to a growl.

Barney's insides felt like broken fruit. Within his chest, gears ground—something was busted in there. The rounds from the Bulldog were no joke, capable of whisking away an arm or leg at close range, and Barney had been caught at less than ten feet. Worse, Erica had manipulated the gun as though she knew what she was doing, not losing her sight picture to the recoil of the first round and plugging all four on target.

She had collected her gun at the bar and concealed it masterfully, or had it planted in the chair cushions the whole time, and yet had pinballed Barney through her idea of an inquisitor's confessional. He was reminded of the way cats toy with still-living prey before sundering it to bloody strings and tatters and a hot spill of exposed organs.

Apparently people paid as little attention to gunshots in a ritzy hotel as they did everywhere else. Erica had waxed Tannenhauser with three neat from the Cobra and dealt Barney four from the Bulldog, no silencers. Cops had never truly existed in Barney's world, and they did not swing in to make everything academic now. Both he and Erica had run out of allies.

They were like an ungainly, multi-limbed alien, spreading one tentacle toward one gun on the floor, then another, flopping about as though in dicey gravity. She did not waste a hand clutching her chest wound and expended her effort on keeping Barney contained as he fought to marshal his own strength.

She swung wildly, trying to punch him in the neck, but he had a crucial few inches of reach on her and her fist fell short. Her tongue was out as she labored to breathe. Unexpectedly he yanked her closer by the throat so he could slam the flat of his other hand into her forehead, right between the eyes. That rocked her badly but she persisted, still full-up with fight. Her shoes had gone flying into a lover's discard on the floor. One was close enough to snatch up and she tried to bury the five-inch, steel-tipped heel into his forebrain. It came down like a hammer and skidded off his temple, excavating a fresh furrow and rebounding off his ear wound. Blistering, molten pain; the right side of his head felt afire.

Barney remembered the gear-up at the Pantera Roja, when the couple had been busily (and vocally) humping in the next room. If there were any neighbors up here on the suite floor, through the walls it probably sounded like more people making big sweaty whoopee. It's what hotels were for: Anonymity behind numbered doors and privacy locks.

So people could kill each other in secret.

Past the green fury in her eyes was a darker taunt: *Why don't you just fuck me and get it over with?*

Barney's grip suddenly went on vacation, as though

his battery for hand-strength had just petered out. Blood was leaking in rivulets down his arm, from under the glove. His traitorous hand released her and she sprawled back, gasping.

He rolled and grabbed the fallen Bulldog with his left hand just as she collected his SIG from the floor.

"Whoops." She said it around a snarl. She pointed the gun at Barney's head and cycled the trigger through a full double-action pull.

Click, nothing.

The ammo in Barney's magazine had indeed come from Armand's dies, but that magazine was in his pocket. Ever since the elevator he had been packing an empty gun. He had known what he was walking into, and had expected to be disarmed on arrival. For the first time, he had not relied upon his own weapon but counted on opportunities in the room as they would reveal themselves—something he had learned in Mexico. He had begun thinking like her, prepared to morph the plan in unexpected ways, since moving in expected ways was what had gotten Sirius and Armand killed.

Erica's mouth popped into an O-shape—as in *oh, you've got to be kidding*—and she actually racked the slide to verify the worst. Empty chamber, vacant clip. It was just enough time, measured in tachycardia, for Barney to swivel on the floor, swing the Bulldog around. The gun was tough black passivate with pancake grips. He pulled the trigger once.

The shot caught her in the cheekbone and the hair on the back of her head flew apart. The slug, a semi-wadcutter, made a ballpoint-pen hole going in. Coming out, it was more like the size of a salad plate. The left

side of her face collapsed around the crush cavity
and her gun hand flew sidewise, drunkenly jettisoning
the SIG.

The Bulldog spent, Barney nonetheless scrambled
on top of her to pin her down. Hemorrhage was already darkening her brow and her eye on the gunshot
side had orbited to a slit of white. Her other eye, still
open, leering green, was fixed on him, but could no
longer see him. No parting *bon mot*, no quip. Just dead.

Feeling pretty dead himself, Barney crawled toward
the bathroom.

The first people to enter the room, later, were Elpidia
Marcos and Esperanza Guitierrez, two Hispanic maids
working for the hotel. They found bodies, blood, guns
and a great deal of folding American currency strewn
around on the bed and floor. Inside the single suitcase
in the bedroom, they found even more money.

By the time they alerted their employers, stories
had been jerry-rigged. Management staff entered the
room to discover bodies, blood, guns and a far smaller
amount of cash strewn around. No suitcase.

By the time the police were summoned, alibis had
been solidified. By the time detectives visited the
by-now thoroughly polluted crime scene, they found
bodies, blood, guns and a couple hundred bucks on
the floor.

The solution that allowed the quickest clean-up was
that the two people in the top-floor suite had murdered
each other with weapons found on-site. This story was
not released to the news media, as the hotel had a reputation to uphold, as well as a fast shuffle in order to
erase all evidence of misdoing and make the room

rentable again as soon as feasible. If someone had suggested a bit of bribery was involved, even in the form of comps and favors to the police, nobody would have laughed.

Barney had left the hotel wearing a dead man's clothing and lugging two suitcases that threatened to pull his tendons out with every step. After patching his ripped ear and realizing there was far too much blood on him to pass without comment, he rifled the closet and found some duds of Tannenhauser's that would pass peripheral scrutiny. He smeared some of Erica's base makeup into his more lurid, visible wounds, then saw that he could not just leave his own bloodsoaked clothing behind, oozing with his DNA. He popped one of the money cases and threw cash in handfuls onto the floor, to make room for the incriminata he had to smuggle out. Fair trade, all things considered.

Down the elevator and through the lobby, the whole trick was not to weave like a drunk, or puke, or black out, or start leaking fresh geysers of the red stuff. Maintain a brisk and businesslike pace. Avoid eye contact. Refuse tip-hungry assistance. Get out, get clear, get free and stay that way.

He made it back to his car, but there was no place for him to go.

Over a thousand people attended the funeral services for the gem-cutter and cowboy geologist known as Mano due to his loss of one hand years before through circumstances shaded in antiquity. Many estimated his age as over a hundred, though in fact he was 95 years old when he died easily, with dignity, surrounded by his many friends and family members in his modest home on the outskirts of the Xochimilco district of Mexico City. It was a neighborhood bordering on the rural, with wide swaths of open land separating grain fields and the occasional small cemetery, all of it yet unspoiled by urban metastasis. The cemetery in which Mano had requested burial had some markers that were nearly double his age, and trees that were four centuries old.

Among the mourners and speakers eulogizing Mano were a contingent of big, brusque men rumored to be luchadors, masked wrestling superstars incognito. Many of them wept openly, yet endured manfully. Tigre Loco, maker of masks, attended in his own distinctive headgear, for no one had ever seen his face, not even his customers.

One individual in particular stood out, mainly because he was taller than most of the mourners; an American who had come to live in Mexico as Mano's apprentice and heir apparent (despite Mano's large and diverse family). This man is referred to by some as *el hombre de las armas*, the gunman, a large, quiet enigma with slender, exotic hands. No one knows his real name, or if he even *has* a name. After his arrival, Mano's gem and jewelry shop was never again targeted by even the most desperate or stupid robbers. Several of Mano's blood relatives now staff the establishment, for when the big man arrived he quickly acquired several vehicles specially outfitted for long excursions deep into the mountains and countryside. He and Mano would often disappear for days on these elaborate expeditions, which grew to possess much of the quality of a vision quest. Nearly always they would bring back some mineral find of rare beauty or astonishing complexity from some dry riverbed or hidden cavern.

They also became a fixture at local cantinas and family-run eateries, always welcome, persistently popular, in no small measure because the mere presence of the stranger was deemed a good thing for the entire community. In the face of indifference by constabularies to petty crime, he seemed to be a guardian angel, like a samurai or paladin, a stoic protector of silent strength who inspired an overall sense of healing. He was the sort of man who has seen enough of pain and suffering and emerged scorched, but not burned, from that crucible. Ordinary people fabricated entire mythologies about his possible past.

Now, with Mano gone, the stranger continues his habit of long treks into the wild, still returning with something compelling every time. He is a frequent visitor and honored backstage guest at Arena Coliseo, where he avidly watches the age-old battle between good and evil enacted by high-flying men in colorful costumes and strange masks, in a ring where alliances are fluid and betrayal is the essence of drama. Good guys, bad guys…and even the most normal person can have a secret identity, an alternate life.

At his workbench in the rear of Mano's shop the stranger labors with a monk's patience among stone tumblers and wax castings, refining the lessons taught by the genteel little man. There is another, larger station for gun work; it takes up an entire wall and features many arcane tools. He has become expert at custom modifications and special adjustments. He manufactures many of his own parts and loads his own special pedigrees of ammunition. In jewelry and stones, he is committed to learning a craft; with guns, he is turning a craft into an artform.

The ghostly entreaties said to be heard at night during the full moon on the Arroyo de La Llorona have been dormant for some time now.

The stranger's odd hands no longer bleed.

Among his many friends are a special group found in the back of his workshop; his closest and most intimate friends, gathered there on the table. You probably already know their names, too: Remington, Ruger, Browning, Beretta, Kimber, Colt, Smith, Wesson, SIG.

By the Edgar Award-Winning Author of
LITTLE GIRL LOST

SONGS of INNOCENCE

by **RICHARD ALEAS**

Three years ago, detective John Blake solved a mystery that changed his life forever—and left a woman he loved dead. Now Blake is back, to investigate the apparent suicide of Dorothy Louise Burke, a beautiful college student with a double life. The secrets Blake uncovers could blow the lid off New York City's sex trade…if they don't kill him first.

Richard Aleas' first novel, LITTLE GIRL LOST, was among the most celebrated crime novels of the year, nominated for both the Edgar and Shamus Awards. *But nothing in John Blake's first case could prepare you for the shocking conclusion of his second…*

RAVES FOR SONGS OF INNOCENCE:

"An instant classic."
— The Washington Post

"The best thing Hard Case is publishing right now."
— The San Francisco Chronicle

"His powerful conclusion will drop jaws."
— Publishers Weekly

"So sharp [it'll] slice your finger as you flip the pages."
— Playboy

To order, visit www.HardCaseCrime.com or call 1-800-481-9191 (10am to 9pm EST).

Each title just $6.99 ($8.99 in Canada), plus shipping and handling.

Get Hard Case Crime by Mail...
And Save 43%!

☐ **YES! Sign me up for the Hard Case Crime Book Club!**

As long as I choose to stay in the club, I will receive every Hard Case Crime book as it is published (generally one each month). I'll get to preview each title for 10 days. If I decide to keep it, I will pay only $3.99* — a savings of 43% off the cover price! There is no minimum number of books I must buy and I may cancel my membership at any time.

Name: _____

Address: _____

City / State / ZIP: _____

Telephone: _____

E-Mail: _____

☐ **I want to pay by credit card:** ☐ VISA ☐ MasterCard ☐ Discover

Card #: _____ Exp. date: _____

Signature: _____

Mail this page to:

HARD CASE CRIME BOOK CLUB
20 Academy Street, Norwalk, CT 06850-4032

Or fax it to 610-995-9274.
You can also sign up online at www.dorchesterpub.com.

* Plus $2.00 for shipping. Offer open to residents of the U.S. and Canada only. Canadian residents please call 1-800-481-9191 for pricing information.

If you are under 18, a parent or guardian must sign. Terms, prices, and conditions subject to change. Subscription subject to acceptance. Dorchester Publishing reserves the right to reject any order or cancel any subscription.